Abandoned

ALSO BY RHONDA POLLERO

The Finding Justice Series
Exposed

The Finley Anderson Tanner Mystery series
Knock Off
Knock em Dead
Fat Chance
Slightly Irregular
Bargain Hunting
No Returns

ABANDONED

RHONDA POLLERO

FOREVER
YOURS

New York   Boston

Copyright © 2017 by Rhonda Pollero
Excerpt from *Trapped* copyright © 2017 by Rhonda Pollero
Cover design by Brian Lemus
Cover copyright © 2017 by Hachette Book Group, Inc.

Forever Yours
Hachette Book Group
1290 Avenue of the Americas
New York, NY 10104
forever-romance.com
twitter.com/foreverromance

First published as an ebook and print on demand edition: June 2017

Forever Yours is an imprint of Grand Central Publishing. The Forever Yours name and logo are trademarks of Hachette Book Group, Inc.

The publisher is not responsible for websites (or their content) that are not owned by the publisher.

The Hachette Speakers Bureau provides a wide range of authors for speaking events. To find out more, go to www.hachettespeakersbureau.com or call (866) 376-6591.

ISBN 978-1-4555-5541-3 (ebook)
ISBN 978-1-4555-9762-8 (print on demand)

For Karen Harrison, my dearest friend,
who knows all of my secrets!

Abandoned

PROLOGUE

The President put one hand at the First Lady's elbow, giving it a brief squeeze before rising to join the governor at the dais. Brilliant light bathed the podium, which was flanked by the most prominent men in Florida politics.

Governor Rossner and his wife applauded politely, as did the dozen or so others basking in the delight of pulling off such an important political coup. Rossner straightened his tie as he turned in his seat and recrossed his legs. *The seat right damned next to the President of the EN-tire U-Nighted friggin' States of America*, he gloated in silence. His barrel chest puffed beneath his suit coat. He wondered what his father would think, him just sitting there with the freakin' most important man in the free world. And that man was about to tell everyone in the crowd that he—Gil Rossner—deserved another term. Stifling his grin, Gil folded his hands in his lap and stared at the president's profile.

He took caution not to catch Maddison's eye. His campaign manager-slash-brother-in-law shared his disdain for the party leader and current commander-in-chief. It simply would not do for the two men to erupt in laughter behind the man's back, though he was sorely tempted. Gil enjoyed belittling the liberal Yankee in the White House.

President Kent Rawlings wasn't much by Gil's standards, yet women seemed to lose their good common sense whenever he was around. His guess was the rumors about Rawlings were true. He stifled a laugh by covering his mouth and quietly clearing his throat. Rawlings was too refined. He and his wife were snobby and polished. Definitely made for television. Gil tried to imagine the prissy man in the sack with that shapely, young First Lady of his. He wondered if the president screamed when he—

Pop!

Gil's eyes bulged as incredible pain seared through him. He slumped slowly to the side. *Sweet Jesus!* were the only words his brain could conjure. There were two more popping sounds. Gil was now lying prone on the floor. A spray of blood blurred his vision. Then he felt crushed beneath a heavy weight as the dead president fell on him. Gil heard his own wife scream as he expelled his final breath.

CHAPTER ONE

TWENTY YEARS LATER

Conner Kavanaugh wasn't normally given to bouts of chivalry, but then there was something decidedly different about the hot blonde currently trying to fend off Frankie's interest. Frankie, an off-duty bartender, may have been born into money, but he was still white trash.

The round stool beneath Conner squealed when he turned back to rest his elbows against the scarred and lacquered bar. He put the long-neck bottle to his lips, taking a long pull and allowing the beer to slide down his throat.

He watched the scene in the mirror behind the bartender. Frankie had one dirty boot on the stool next to the blonde. His hat was pushed back on his head. To her credit, the blonde wasn't even looking at him. Conner snorted and took another sip of his beer. She was obviously thinking that subtlety would work on a guy like Frankie, but Conner knew better. Frankie didn't comprehend anything less subtle than a two-by-four against his temple.

She didn't exactly fit the type of woman who came trolling at The Grill. First off, her clothes were all wrong. Her Harvard sweatshirt was loose enough to cover all but the faintest outline of her breasts. *And those jeans*, he thought as he took another pull of beer. Though they were faded from wear, the material held a distinct crease—a dry-cleaners crease, he figured with an amused shake of his head. *Well, at least she had spruced up her fanciest duds for her night out.*

When she finally lifted her eyes, he felt the impact as if he'd been slapped. Even in the smoky haze of the bar, they were the greenest he'd ever seen. Clear, emerald green. And shimmering with anger.

Frankie apparently wasn't seeing it that way. Conner watched the large man anchor himself on the stool as he pushed it just inches from his quarry. *Why*, he wondered, *couldn't this broad have picked a safer place to find Mr. Right Now?* With her looks she could have sauntered up to the Dairy Queen and found someone eager to spend the night with her. *Maybe she liked slumming*, he considered as he finished off his drink. He watched as Frankie continued to move in on her. The man had less finesse than a teenager on prom night in the front seat of his father's pickup. His big palm gripped her wrist, wrestling her hand to his sloppy mouth.

The woman's eyes narrowed, but she didn't seem to put up much of a fight. Conner's chivalrous thoughts were dismissed when he realized he'd been wrong. "Happens," he muttered with a shrug. Some women just liked 'em nasty.

He'd no sooner turned his attention away from them when he heard the familiar sound of a bottle being smashed. "Damn!" he sighed. He was off duty and he sure as hell wasn't in any mood to break up a drunken bar fight.

Expecting to find a couple of townies squared off by the pool tables, he looked there first. It wasn't the townies. He shifted his gaze in the opposite direction. It wasn't Frankie. No, the hand holding the jagged glass weapon belonged to the Harvard blonde.

"You gonna do something?" the bartender fairly pleaded.

"Think I should?" Conner countered without taking his eyes off the standoff. "It's my night off," he mentioned almost casually.

"C'mon," Bart groaned. "I can't afford no more fights in here. Councilman Tuppman and his holier-than-thou wife are just itching for a reason to get my liquor license pulled. Anybody gets hurt, I can kiss this place good-bye."

Now *that* would be a loss, Conner thought as he slowly got to his feet. His boots scraped the worn floor as he closed the space between himself and where Frankie stood, apparently ready to pounce on the woman or the weapon she brandished—or both.

Conner slipped his hand onto Frankie's tense shoulder. A small semi-circle of interested folks gathered around the participants.

"You don't want to get into a brawl with a woman, do

you, Frankie? It sure would give Tarrant County a bad name." Conner kept his eyes on the weapon.

"You gonna let that bitch get the best of you?" someone taunted.

"Yeah, Frankie!" another voice echoed. "Can't be letting no woman kick your ass!"

"Take that bottle away from her, Frankie!" someone else called. "Show her what a real man does when a woman gets outta line!"

Conner knew 'ol Frankie would rise to the bait. Frankie was one of those individuals destined to spend his entire life being goaded by others. His past was testimony to that. His father had been leading him around by the nose for years. It didn't seem to matter that Frankie was pushing forty-three.

"You really don't want to do that, Frankie," Conner said calmly. "Doesn't take much of a man to beat up on a little thing like her."

Now Frankie turned and snarled at him with eyes that were narrow and angry—just like the guy's brain. Amazingly, the Harvard blonde was shooting *him* a pretty hostile look as well. Apparently, everyone was having a bad day.

Frankie snarled. "This ain't your concern, Kavanaugh." He puffed out his muscled chest and added, "'Sides, you're in no position to tell me what to do in here."

Conner sighed. "I see it a little differently," he countered. "My mamma was real clear on the rules about boys hitting girls."

"Your mamma was a whore," Frankie spat.

Conner's first response was an audible, deep sigh. "Frankie,

I don't think you want to make me mad just now. Do you?"

Conner saw a faint flicker of uncertainty pass in the smaller man's eyes. "You don't scare me, Kavanaugh. Never have, never will."

"I'm not trying to scare you. I'm trying to reason with you. Surely you have something better to do tonight than pick a fight with a girl."

"Girl?" the Harvard blonde scoffed.

The broken bottle never wavered from her target, not even when she tossed some of that long, thick hair over one shoulder. "I am *not* a girl. I don't know why you feel the need to play Knight in Shining Armor, but I can assure you, I'm perfectly capable of taking care of myself."

Conner grinned. "That must be why you're standing in the middle of a barroom full of sloppy-drunk men with a broken bottle in your hand."

She stiffened with indignation and he wished he had just stayed out of the whole situation. "Suit yourself, sweetheart. Sorry for interrupting your fun."

Her eyes burned like fire as she glared at him.

"Go on, Frankie!" one of the men yelled as Conner began to move backward toward the bar. "Teach her some manners!"

Conner had every intention of leaving her to her own devices: let her learn a small lesson so long as it didn't get truly bad. That lasted only until he saw the smallest flicker of fear on her face. He should have ignored it. She had basically told him as much. He should have let the foolish woman get her due. Lord knew she'd asked for it by coming to a place like this and giving Frankie the time of day. But as he thought about her small body being manhandled by a pig like Frankie, he knew he was going to help her. Even if she didn't want him to.

"I'm sure you're right capable of taking care of yourself," he began as he stepped between her and Frankie. "But I wouldn't be much of a gentleman if I—"

He hadn't finished the sentence when he felt an explosion in the area of his ribs. His breath billowed in his cheeks. He heard the Harvard blonde's sharp shriek. He was almost sorry that Frankie hadn't decided to sucker-punch him in the mouth. At least then he would have had the satisfaction of bleeding all over the dim-witted woman. As far as he was concerned, this whole situation was her fault.

"That," he warned Frankie between clenched teeth, "wasn't real smart."

With a speed belying his size, Conner caught the other man around the mid-section in a move that sent them spraying atop the pool table. Bracing his forearm across Frankie's throat, Conner turned and glanced at the blonde. He caught a faint whiff of her perfume. Annoyed at the world in general and at her specifically, he asked, "May I borrow your bottle, please?"

Stunned, the woman relinquished it to his free hand. Ignoring her for the moment, Conner stared down at the menacing, red face of his opponent. The room had gone still and silent. He was able to hear every rasp of breath. Conner placed the jagged edge of the bottle to the base of Frankie's throat.

"This ain't your fight, Kavanaugh," Frankie gasped in a whisper.

Conner eased his pressure hold on the man. "I beg to differ." He allowed the glass to pierce Frankie's sweaty skin. "You threw the first punch."

"But I didn't mean no harm."

"Sure." Conner put more weight into his hold. The action caused Frankie's watered-down blue eyes to bulge in their sockets. "I don't take kindly to having my ribs punched."

Frankie's thin lips pulled back to expose two rows of capped teeth. He managed to shrug defeat from beneath Conner's hold and the threat of the jagged glass.

Conner moved close to the man's ear. "When I let you up, you'll head on out the door. Understand?"

Frankie was glaring, but he nodded. Somehow, Conner didn't find his attitude very reassuring. He decided Frankie might need just a bit more persuasion. Bracing one leg firmly on the floor, he brought his knee up and applied attention-getting pressure to Frankie's crotch. "I didn't catch your answer."

The combination of the bottle against his jugular, the band of muscle against his throat, and the distinct threat to his privates, apparently made Frankie see the error of his ways.

"I didn't really want that frosty bitch anyways," Frankie puffed, casting his eyes in the direction of the woman. "I like my women a whole hell of a lot softer than her."

"Then there won't be a problem," Conner acknowledged. Slowly, he eased off the man, but kept the broken bottle raised just in case Frankie got another attack of the stupids. He knew from prior experience that ninety percent of Frankie's decision-making was fifty-percent stupid.

Luckily, this wasn't one of those times. Conner placed himself and the weapon between the Harvard blonde and Frankie while the latter collected his hat. Shoving through the visibly disappointed group of men, Frankie stomped out of the bar. Expelling a breath, Conner had a sinking suspicion this wasn't quite over. Frankie was short on brains but long on memory.

Absently, he kneaded his ribs, relieved when he felt only mildly uncomfortable. Cracked ribs were a pain in the ass. Speaking of pains in the ass…He turned, wanting an explanation from Miss Harvard Blonde.

What she apparently lacked in common sense, she definitely had in looks. He felt the beginnings of a smile. Her hair was beautiful, spilling well below her shoulders in a simple, no-frills style. Judging from the way she had smashed the beer bottle to challenge a man twice her size, Conner assumed her hair was simply an extension of her personality—blunt.

"Come here often?" he remarked casually.

She regarded him with something amazingly akin to defiance. He could see it in the subtle thrust of her chin and the small fists balled at her sides.

"You didn't need to come to my rescue," she responded tightly.

Her accent was southern, but not North Florida southern.

"I could have controlled the situation."

"It didn't look like that from where I was sitting," he told her. Hell, he didn't expect her to fall into his arms and kiss him with gratitude, but it annoyed him that she couldn't so much as say thanks. She owed him that. She could at least show him the courtesy of civility.

"You could have hurt him."

Was that censure he heard in her tone? "Excuse me?"

Her hands moved to her hips. "The broken bottle would have allowed me to make a quick, gracious exit. There was no need for you to hold it against his throat and incite a fight."

His blood pressure went up a notch or two. "I *prevented* a fight, sweetheart."

"Not from where I was sitting," she returned in a near-perfect imitation of his drawl.

"This is crazy!"

"No," she countered. "*You're* crazy."

She breezed past him as if he was nothing more than a minor annoyance. A gnat she might swat, had she been so inclined to donate some of her precious time.

The few men who still lingered parted as if she was royalty. Of course, given the regal way she swayed her tight little derrière, it didn't surprise him. It just made him madder than hell.

"Wait a minute!"

Her step faltered at his thunderous command but she still pushed the door open and walked out into the night. He should just leave this alone. Chalk it up to a good deed for which he would eventually be rewarded. But he didn't feel much like waiting for eventually. She owed him, and he believed in collecting on his debts.

Depositing the broken bottle on the bar as he strode by, Conner stormed after her. Like it or not, the woman was going to get his short lesson on manners.

Cool, fresh air welcomed him as he stepped from The Grill. It took him less than a second to find her. It was easy. He simply followed the chirping sound made as she disarmed her Lexus in the dark parking lot.

She really is slumming, he grumbled inwardly as he jogged over to her car. He got there just in time to see her settle in behind the wheel and blocked the closing of her car door with his body.

When she angled her head up at him, Conner felt his annoyance double at the exasperation plainly visible in the tiny lines at the corners of her full lips.

"Stop being a jerk," she warned, impatient.

"A jerk?" he parroted.

"Okay," she amended, batting her long lashes at him. "Stop being a complete asshole."

Her condescension didn't bother him so much as her voice. This woman had a cultured cadence, the kind of speech pattern learned only in the finest schools. It was the kind of speech that didn't usually include the names and expletives she had so easily tossed at him.

"If I'm such an asshole, how come you're looking to get laid in a dive like this?"

She blinked once. "And who told you I was looking to get *laid*, as you so coarsely put it?"

"Why else would a woman like *you* come to a place like *this?*"

"For a beer?" she suggested.

"Were they all out at the country club?"

"I've got news for you," she said as she reached for the door handle. "I don't belong to any country clubs, but I do enjoy a beer now and again."

"I would suggest you enjoy it someplace other than here."

"Oh, I get it!" she said in a breathy, sarcastic rush. "This is one of those quaint 'men only' places."

"You could say that."

She gave him an exaggerated dumb-blonde sigh. "Gee, I guess I should have checked the corners of the building for urine. Isn't that how most lower animal species mark their territory?"

Conner chuckled. She was quick. "Would you have liked it better if I would have let 'ol Frankie have you?"

"Frankie would not have *had* me."

"There's not a whole lot of you, sweetheart. That bottle trick would have protected you for a while, but not forever. Frankie and his friends would have seen to that."

"Perhaps," she said. "But I still believe I could have handled it myself."

Placing his palms on the polished roof of the fancy car, Conner leaned down. The red interior of the car smelled new. She smelled fresh, like the air after a shower.

"I'm willing to concede that you might have been able to pull it off, if you're willing to concede that it was damned neighborly of me to intervene on your behalf."

Her lashes fluttered against her cheeks. The action caused his body to respond with alarming speed. Her skin was pale, flawless, and slightly flushed from the cool evening air. She was a tiny thing but the word "vulnerable" didn't even enter his mind.

She hesitated, then said, "Okay. Thank you for being neighborly, Mr.—"

"Conner Kavanaugh. Conner to my friends."

"Mr. Kavanaugh," she said. A small smile curved the corners of her mouth.

"And you are?"

"About to leave," she answered, gently tugging on the door.

Ignoring the feel of metal against the backs of his calves, Conner remained planted in the spot. "I'd like to know your name. Telling me would be the neighborly thing for you to do."

"I guess I'm just not as neighborly as you are." Some of the annoyance had returned to her eyes.

"I don't know," he drawled. "You impress me as a lady with potential." Conner gave her his best grin. The one that had talked his fair share of women out of their panties.

She looked as volatile as a fast-approaching tornado. "Potential?"

He nodded. "Knew it the minute I set eyes on you."

The lips he'd been admiring pulled into a tight smile.

"I get it. You're under the impression that since you defended my honor—so to speak—I'm now fair game?"

"I'm game if you are," he teased, hoping to get her to lighten up.

"I hate to disappoint you," she said in a tone that told him she didn't mind disappointing him at all.

"I wasn't interested in spoils," he insisted.

"And I'm not interested, *period.*"

"Sure you are," he told her without conceit. "Or your eyes wouldn't be flickering between my face and my—"

"My eyes have not flickered."

Her voice was stiff and haughty. Still he sensed just a trace of wariness behind her brave words. The lady wasn't as immune as she was letting on. That knowledge filled him with a hefty dose of male pride.

"Suit yourself. But I'd be right flattered if they did." Conner moved and she closed the door. She surprised him when she lowered the window.

"You're either desperate or a bigger jerk than I originally thought."

"Careful, sweetheart," he said as his fingers reached out to brush the soft underside of her chin. Her skin was silky soft and he wondered what the rest of her body felt like. He also wondered why she hadn't so much as flinched at the contact. Perhaps this lady liked games. Specifically the "convince me" game. "You don't want to hurt my feelings, do you?"

"I really don't give a flaming hoot about your feelings, Kavanaugh."

His fingers traced the delicate outline of her throat until he encountered the edge of her collar. His eyes followed his hands, inspiring all sorts of fantasies.

Then he heard an unmistakable *click.*

His gaze moved toward the sound. His fingers stilled as

he found himself looking down the barrel of a small-caliber gun.

"Take your hand off me," she said calmly.

The fingers gripping the gun were as steady as her gaze. Conner wondered how he had managed to get himself into such a mess. *So much for chivalry*, he thought as he slowly pulled his hand back. He knew the answer; he'd been thinking with the wrong part of his anatomy. *Stupid.*

"Do you always use a gun as persuasion?" He was careful to keep his tone conversational. Apparently she didn't like that. He could tell by the flash of surprise in her eyes. She must have thought her little Annie Oakley moment would have had a more intimidating effect. Of course, he still wasn't sure she wouldn't shoot, but he'd gnaw off his own tongue before admitting that to her.

"If you'll recall, Kavanaugh, I asked you nicely first."

"I guess I wasn't listening right," he said, stepping away from the car.

He heard her start the engine. She propped the gun on the window frame. Her eyes never left him. Not for an instant.

"Perhaps in the future you'll remember that *no* actually means *no*."

CHAPTER TWO

Damn it to hell." This was the second time Emma McKinley had had to wipe off and redo the eyeliner on her left eye. "Come on!" The more she hurried so she wasn't late for her first day, the more she screwed up her makeup and had to start over. "Breathe. Less haste, more speed." Good pep talk.

It was nearly eight o'clock by the time she finished dicking around with her makeup. Standing back from the full-length mirror, she gave herself a critical head-to-toe, toe-to-head inspection; Makeup—after three attempts—perfect. She'd chosen the pale gray suit and soft white silk blouse with calculating care the night before. She knew how to play the game. Two years in the Manhattan P.D.'s Office, followed by the fiasco at Gunderson-Halloway and Belk had served as excellent training. After New York, this backwater place in Florida would be like returning to kindergarten.

She'd woven her streaky blond, shoulder-length hair into a neat, efficient French braid. Classic, classy, and businesslike, she expected to be taken seriously. Looking professional was a lesson she'd learned long before graduation. Contrary to its public appearance, the legal system, in many ways, was more sexist and elitist than the real world.

In order to play down her looks, she followed a few simple rules. No bows of any kind, anywhere. No jewelry, except for her watch. Minimal cosmetic enhancements—liner and a touch of blush, some mascara and a hint of gloss on her lips.

Definitely no perfume. It was a Catch-22. If she smelled like a cosmetic counter, her credibility stunk. But this was her reality. A reality she detested.

Minutes later, keys dangling from between her teeth, she carried a travel mug of hazelnut coffee and her briefcase in one hand as she pulled the door closed behind her with the other. An insect chirp hung in the cool, already muggy, early morning air. A low-level mist floated just above the ground, making her secluded lawn and drive look like a dry ice special effect. There was a fragrance in the late March breeze; something sweet that could have come from any of the dozen or so flowers battling for space in her untended flowerbeds.

"Note to self," she said after taking her keys from her mouth. "Get a book on gardening after unpacking the house."

Emma slipped into her racing-red Lexus. The car was just one of her trophies. *More like a consolation prize*, she acknowledged as she started down the still-unfamiliar streets of Purdue. For some reason, her victory over Gunderson-Halloway and Belk didn't seem to matter so much anymore. Grimacing as she swallowed, she made another note to self: "Find someplace that sells coffee without chicory!" Even the hazelnut flavoring she'd added couldn't mask the bitterness.

Located northeast of Tampa, the town was home to about seven thousand residents. It was nestled in the swamps and bayous that few people thought of when they thought of Florida. No, most people thought sandy beaches or Disney magic—but in truth, North Florida was mostly pine swamp and was more like Louisiana than the postcard version of Florida.

Emma was definitely an outsider. Being raised in the north Georgia mountains wouldn't count for much in these parts. The townsfolk of Purdue were proud of their land, their heritage, and their secrets. Well, she thought as she pulled into the rutted parking lot adjacent to the Purdue Municipal Building, she might just have to do something about those secrets.

Her attaché case was more for show, as much of a prop as her tailored suit. The heels of her gunmetal pumps clicked a melodic rhythm against the polished, square-tiled floor of the building's lobby. Every time the exterior door opened, cigarette smoke joined the smell of musty papers, bacon, and stale coffee.

A rotund man in his mid- to late fifties sat perched on a stool just inside the lobby. The floor beneath his feet was scuffed, indicating he might have occupied that exact post since the dawn of time. An overhead light reflected off the small bald circle at his crown. Reading his name tag, Emma offered a polite smile.

"Good morning, Mr. Posten, I'm Emma McKinley."

"The new girl," he stated with a nod.

Swallowing the annoying memory of Kavanaugh calling her a girl, she said, "I have an 8:30 meeting with Elgin Hale."

"Take the elevator to the third floor. Double doors will be to your left." He flipped his head in the general direction, then went back to reading his newspaper.

She felt Posten's small, brown eyes on her back as she walked away. She wondered if she could expect the same sort of politically incorrect treatment from all the men in Purdue. She hoped not; she'd already slayed the dragon of the narrow-minded power brokers in New York. If she had to do that again, she'd probably opt instead for a quick falling on her sword.

The upper floor of the building was only slightly more plush than the lobby. The carpet was a godawful shade of beige, but it was clean and cushiony beneath her feet. Hearing no sounds as she made her way down the narrow hall, she passed about five closed doors inscribed with names of assistants in the office before she got to the one marked RE-CEPTION.

At the very end of the hallway, she found her target. ELGIN HALE, COUNTY PUBLIC DEFENDER was painted on the center panel of a set of massive doors. The gold paint was beginning to flake.

She peered into the office but saw no signs of life. Sucking in a breath of fortification, Emma knocked three times.

Nothing.

She tried again; this time she put more force behind the action.

Still nothing.

Irritation rumbled in her empty stomach. The man had said 8:30 sharp. So where was he? To her, tardiness was a freaking sign of rudeness.

Grabbing the polished brass knob, she was a little startled to find the door unlocked and pushed it open.

A large, cluttered, rectangular desk covered with listing stacks of file folders dominated the office. A multi-line telephone sat dormant. A dated computer and its peripherals sat on a nicked credenza behind the desk. The rest of the space was devoted to a montage of photographs. The faint smell of Old Spice hung in the air.

"Hello?" she called. There were two closed doors on the far side of the room.

"Damn it, Bill!" she heard a male voice yell. "Can't your wife stay home today? I can't be in two places at one time. The new chick starts today!"

A chick and a girl. Emma checked her watch. *And all before nine in the morning. This day just gets better and better.* Plastering a smile on her face, Emma knocked on the bellower's door. "C'mon in, Jenny," he barked. "And I hope you've got the coffee started. Oh, and let me know when that bro—"

Crossed at the ankles, his sock-covered feet were perched on the edge of the desk. He'd been tapping them to some unheard tune as she stepped through the door. Elgin Hale, phone cradled between his shoulder and ear, stared at her with his mouth open. His blue eyes fixed on her face.

Pulling the receiver away from his mouth, he asked, "What can I do for you, honey?"

Chick, girl, honey? Didn't anyone in Tarrant County understand political correctness and/or basic feminist protocol? "I'm Emma McKinley."

Hale lowered his legs and she heard noises suggesting he had found his shoes. One large hand fumbled with the receiver, then he sat straight in his leather swivel chair. "Right, Bill," he said into the phone. "See what you can work out and call me back." There was a pause, then he said, "Make it quick. Judge Crandall isn't likely to grant a postponement on this one. You know him. Call back when you've gotten your shit together."

While Hale finished his call, Emma deposited her attaché and purse in one seat, then sat in the other directly across from her about-to-be new boss. Her eyes scanned the walls behind him. Generic undergraduate degree, generic law school, and none of the gold and black magna cum laude ribbons that edged her own diplomas. However, the man across from her had a decent reputation. She knew; she'd checked before making the trip to Purdue. Not that his credentials made any difference to her decision.

He could have had a degree from eBay. She'd still have come. In his twenty-plus years in practice, Hale had earned some amount of respect among his peers. There were several framed commendations as well as some framed news articles praising him cluttering his walls. Most of the frames were crocked, and all of them were dusty.

"Miss McKinley." He rose from behind his desk and stretched out a beefy hand. "Glad to finally meet you."

"Thank you." She shook his outstretched hand. Pleasantly, she added, "Though it sounds as if you'd be happier if I was Bill."

His weathered face softened under a smile. Expelling a breath of frustration, Hale explained. "Bill has a full court calendar and a kid with the chicken pox. He says it's his turn to stay home. Christ," Hale groaned, then ran his stubby fingers through the shock of his thick, white hair. "What the hell ever happened to a mother staying home with her sick kid?"

A new century? Emma thought, yet held her tongue.

Shuffling through a stack on his desk, Hale extracted a file and set it in front of him. Without looking up he asked, "You don't have kids, do you?"

"No." *But thanks for asking question number one on the "Do not ask applicants this question" list.*

She listened to the ticking of a naval clock perched on an overcrowded bookcase as Hale continued to shuffle files and papers. His brows were drawn together when he looked up at her. Meeting her eyes, he half-asked, half-said, "Larry Grisom recommended you for this job?"

"Yes. Larry was one of my professors in law school. He taught several courses on criminal law."

"At Harvard?" His tone was a blend of admiration and mild amusement. "Larry should be in a courtroom, not a classroom."

She nodded. "He was a wonderful litigator. I learned a lot from him."

"Then if you don't mind my asking, why is a Harvard grad who—according to your résumé—did a great job for the New York Public Defender's Office and a swanky New York defense firm interested in a low-paying job as an assistant PD in Purdue?"

"I'm something of a pariah in New York these days. I came to Purdue to practice law. It's something I do very well."

"So I read," Hale acknowledged. "But why here?"

"Why not?" she responded. She punctuated her answer with a bright smile she hoped would end the mini-inquisition.

"Fair enough," he said, reclining to stroke the second of his three chins.

He sized her up. The PD may have donned the relaxed air of a simple country lawyer, but the clear intelligence she read in his eyes belied the façade.

"Then," Hale began as he dove into the stacks of files, "since you're here and Bill isn't, you can take care of this." He passed her a rather thin file. "You have been admitted to the Florida State Bar, right?"

"Last week," she informed him.

Hale stood. "The courthouse is across the street. You'll find your client in the basement floor holding cell. Judge Crandall takes the bench at ten. Calls the first case at ten-o-one."

* * *

Six minutes later, she was on her way to meet her first client. The courthouse was a stately old building with iron railings and Georgian columns. It was warm inside, making Emma wonder what it would be like in the heat of summer.

With any luck, I won't be here in the summer.

After she displayed her credentials to him, a tall, young deputy escorted her down into what he called the "dungeon." The name was apt. The air was stagnant and damp. It smelled like an old tennis shoe. Following him down the cinderblock, canyonlike hall, Emma tuned out the muffled voices from the prisoners within the locked, dank cells.

She was walking and reading at the same time. Luckily the case file was thin—just a charging document, some letters, copies of the arresting officer's report, and a docket sheet.

The deputy ushered her into one of the cells. Emma was instantly struck by the appearance of the person seated at the chipped Formica table. He had dark hair falling over one eye, and a soft new growth of fuzz above his lip and in patches around his chin. He had the look of youthful innocence, like he should be the poster child for some skateboard manufacturer. He didn't look like a criminal, but then she knew how deceiving appearance could be.

Tossing his head back, he treated Emma to an insolent smile. But she saw a trace of curiosity behind the bravado. "Who are you?"

She dismissed the deputy. "Emma McKinley. I'm your court-appointed attorney. I'll be defending you."

"You?" he scoffed, tilting his chair so it balanced on the back two legs.

"Bill's kid has the chicken pox, so you're stuck with me. Is there some problem with that"—she paused to consult the file—"David?"

The Segan boy shrugged his lanky, seventeen-year-old shoulders with forced disinterest. "Depends on if you're any good."

"There are people who think I'm an exceptional attorney," she answered blandly. She read his arrest record and the most recent letter from the State's Attorney. "The State is willing to lower the charge against you to a misdemeanor if you'll name your drug supplier."

"Right," David sneered. "You aren't from around here, are you?"

"No." She met his gaze. "Does that make a difference?"

"If you were a local girl, you would understand how it is."

Okay, maybe I can make some headway with Purdue's next generation. "Don't call me a girl ever again. You think I don't understand the ramifications of you taking the plea offer?"

"Right the first time."

She rolled her eyes. "This may be a small town, but I'm pretty familiar with your situation. I'm guessing that if you rat on your friends, then you won't have any friends. And you don't want to be where you aren't wanted, right?"

"Yep," David agreed. His initial tough guy exterior began

to fade. "'Sides, it really was the first time I ever tried to score any weed."

And pigs fly. "So you just had the misfortune of committing your first felony in front of Deputy…Hammond?"

"He's an ass," David slurred with derision.

"He may be an ass. Don't know and I don't much care. But you aren't in any position to be calling anyone an ass. You were the one lame enough to be caught buying a bag of sale-weight grass at nine in the morning." She met his gaze. "Are you a user?"

David averted his eyes and gripped his soda can tightly. There was a large black bruise beneath the nail of the thumb he was using to trace the outline of the soda's logo.

"Are you?"

"Not really. I mean, sometimes I use…recreationally."

"Want to know how many people I've met that were 'recreational' drug abusers at seventeen and dead by twenty?"

"What are you? My lawyer or a fucking DFS social worker?"

She fished in her purse for her glasses. It was a stall tactic. So David was acquainted with the Department of Family Services. She put on her glasses and answered. "Your lawyer. Which is why I need to know these things." She flipped through his arrest record. "You've got some Juvie fines for loitering, truancy, runaway, and a trespass on government property."

"Told you I wasn't a druggie," he retorted, crossing his arms in front of his shirt.

"Then you shouldn't dress like one," she suggested. She noticed him flinch out of the corner of her eye. His black DEATH RULES T-shirt and grunge-style jeans wouldn't exactly curry favor with the judge. "Is anyone bringing you clothes?"

Her question shattered the pretense of toughness. David's insolent eyes lowered as he took a sip of his drink. "No one I know is particularly interested in my appearance, Miss McKinley."

Checking her watch, Emma knew there wasn't enough time to spruce her client up before court.

Strike one.

"What about school?"

"Bailed last year."

Strike two.

"Work?"

His defiant expression returned. "Nothing yet. I'm holding out for something with decent health insurance and a 401K plan."

Strike three, he's out. Closing the file, Emma said, "If you're bright enough to know what a retirement plan is, then you should be bright enough to find a job."

His chair came forward with a resounding thud. "It isn't all that easy here in Purdue. This isn't Tampa or Miami, Miss McKinley."

"I'm sure it isn't easy, but that isn't an excuse for not trying to do something with your life."

"Jeez, lady!" he griped. "Mr. Whitley didn't lecture me when he came here."

"What did he do?" Emma asked.

"He said I should take the deal."

"Then what?"

David blinked.

"Then what were you going to do?" she pressed.

He shrugged and crossed his arms on top of the table. This time he traced the obscenity carved into the tabletop. "I guess I'll go on doing what I've been doing."

Frustrated, Emma snapped, "Listen, Rebel-Without-A-Clue. You're too old to play these idiotic games." She shot him a look designed to convey her disgust with his childish behavior. "I have a personal policy never to waste my time on idiots."

She stood, gathered her papers, briefcase, and purse. Her glasses dangled between her thumb and forefinger. "I'll see you upstairs where you will *not* take the plea and probably be found guilty."

"Wait!" David yelled as soon as she turned her back.

"What will happen to me? Mr. Whitley said Judge Crandall would send me to Jarrettsville if I got convicted."

"He was right. I'm guessing at least a five-year sentence."

"Can't you do anything?" David fairly pleaded.

She turned back to him. "I'll help you on one condition."

"Get a job, right?" David moaned.

She shook her head. "Your promise that you'll get a life, David. You're seventeen and smart. I function much better as an advocate if I know I'm helping someone who wants to help himself."

"So I take the plea and rat out my friends."

"They aren't your friends," Emma answered. "And you're not taking a plea."

"What are you going to do?"

"You'll see," Emma said, smiling at him before leaving.

If she was very, very lucky, David would reevaluate his situation before they went before the judge.

* * *

It was not so different than the other courtrooms she'd entered. Walking briskly and with confidence, she pushed through the wooden gate that separated the spectators from the litigants and placed her items on the trial table. The elevated bench loomed in front of her, a U.S. flag and a state flag guarding over the currently unoccupied, high-backed chair. She was vaguely aware of a din of whispered voices behind her and the open curiosity from the man standing at the prosecution table.

Emma, as was her custom, made the first move.

She introduced herself to the man in the pale blue suit. The smile he offered in return was authentic. And it testified to the man's long-term adolescent visits with an orthodontist.

"Hayden Blackwell," he stated as he took her outstretched hand. "I heard rumors that Elgin was bringing in some new blood."

"Nice to meet you, too."

Hayden released her hand and pointed a finger-made gun at her. "Great to have a pretty face across the aisle. You don't sound like you're a local girl."

Battling to keep her smile in place, Emma simply said, "Georgia."

"I have people in Georgia. Whereabouts are you from?"

Emma was relieved when the bailiff entered to announce the start of the session so she didn't have to answer the question.

Moving back to her table, she felt the interest of the handful or so spectators seated in the gallery. Then the bailiff announced court was in session.

Judge Crandall entered the courtroom with the black sleeves of his judicial robe fluttering. He had a regal air about him, one that seemed in perfect harmony with his distinguished looks. Emma put him somewhere in the vicinity of sixty, and he was tall and slender, with just a hint of his white shirt and paisley tie visible at the neckline of his robe. His eyes were dark, his expression stern and authoritative. The only break in his taciturn expression came after he was seated. When his eyes focused on her.

"Good morning," he said in a voice that easily carried to the back of the room. "Where is Mr. Whitley, young lady?"

"Chicken pox, Your Honor," Emma replied as a side door opened and David shuffled in with shackles connecting his wrists and ankles. Seeing her client in chains made her angry. No wonder the kid rebelled against the system. Emma wondered how many of the good 'ol boys would enjoy being hog-tied and paraded around in public.

"Bill has the chicken pox?" the judge asked.

"One of his children, I believe. I filed the Notice of Substitution with your clerk on my way in. Emma McKinley,

Your Honor. Attorney of record for David Segan."

The judge shook his head. "The new gal," the judge commented as he lifted his gavel.

"Wayne," the judge said to the bailiff, "let the games begin." The gavel came down and made a thunderous noise that echoed in the courtroom. Emma looked at her watch. Exactly one minute after ten.

David fell into the seat next to hers. She gripped his upper arm, forcing him to stand. "Wipe that smartass look off your face and behave," she whispered.

David jerked his arm free, but his expression instantly turned less hostile.

Wayne, the bailiff, read the charges into the record before the judge looked to Emma.

"Plea?"

"Not guilty."

"Motion for jury?"

"Waived, Your Honor," Emma replied.

Her answers were followed by a series of whispers and a definitely shocked look from her adversary.

"Proceed, then, Mr. Blackwell. Opening remarks?"

Blackwell recovered quickly, but that was to be expected. She listened as he addressed the court, explaining that David Segan had been caught red-handed by Deputy Hammond out at someplace called Jonah's Launch.

When he was finished, Emma reserved her right to make a statement to the court.

"The state calls Deputy Curtis Hammond."

A huge man with a chest as large as her first apartment

in New York waddled up to the stand. His uniform was starched and cleaned, save for dark perspiration stains when he lifted his arm to take the oath. A dirty-brimmed hat was clamped in his pudgy left hand. He held his other hand on the butt of his gun as he climbed into the witness box.

Hearing the nervous jingle of David's leg irons, Emma leaned over and whispered, "You're right; the deputy does look like an ass."

David snickered and the jingling stopped.

"Deputy, did you have occasion to observe the defendant out at Jonah's Launch on three January of this year?"

"David and them other hellraisers—"

"Objection!" Emma called politely, rising from her seat. "The witness is characterizing the defendant for the court."

"Sustained. Try to keep it simple, will you, Curtis?"

A reddish blotch appeared on the throat of the deputy as he glared over at her.

"I saw the defendant at the edge of the pier with three other...*individuals.*"

"And what," Blackwell asked, "if anything, did you observe?"

"I moved closer to them because I figured they were up to no good."

"Objection!" Emma called out without standing.

"Sustained," the judge concurred.

This time the glare came her way via the State's Attorney.

"Did you observe anything that caused you to be suspicious?"

"The defendant handed one of the other individuals a

folded bill. Then the same individual handed the defendant a full bag of marijuana."

"Objection," Emma rose slowly, the pads of her fingertips rested on counsel table. "The witness is testifying about matters not yet in evidence. Further, Mr. Blackwell has failed to lay a proper foundation for—"

The judge sighed with displeasure. "Do us all a favor, Mr. Blackwell. Move the contraband into evidence so we can get on with this."

Blackwell lowered his head briefly, then confessed, "There has been an irregularity with the evidence, Your Honor."

"Such as?" the judge prompted.

Blackwell rubbed his forehead and said, "When Deputy Hammond went back to the station with the defendant, he was speaking with the sheriff while the defendant used the restroom. The defendant disposed of the evidence in the, uh, toilet."

"Objection!" Emma stated firmly. "The State's Attorney is testifying."

The judge ran his fingertips over his neatly trimmed hair. Deputy Hammond looked like he'd enjoy nothing more than to rip his gun from his belt and shoot her on the spot.

"Further," Emma continued. "In light of the fact that the State can't possibly prove its *prima facie* case without the narcotic allegedly seized at the time of the arrest, the defense moves for an immediate dismissal."

"For Christ's sake," Hammond grumbled from the stand.

"Mr. Blackwell?" the judge prodded.

"The State believes that this witness, who actually had

possession of the narcotic for a time, has sufficient expertise to—"

Emma took a deep, deliberate breath. "Objection, Your Honor. The State has offered no foundation for establishing this witness as an expert in controlled substances."

"*Everybody* knows what dope smells like, lady!" Hammond insisted, irritated and turning redder as the seconds passed.

"Well," the judge drawled, "Not *everybody* was responsible for securing the evidence, Curtis. Just you."

"Ask the sheriff!" Hammond argued. "He saw it on his desk before that little nose-wipe flushed it in the can!"

Judge Crandall looked over Emma's head and asked, "Well, Sheriff?"

Curious to see if the sheriff was Laurel to Hammond's Hardy, Emma turned her head. Her breath caught when he rose, whisking off his hat in one smooth movement.

Ebony hair spilled on to his forehead, falling just shy of the most intense gray eyes she had ever seen. He was even more attractive than she had originally thought. But this was the first time she had seen him in decent light. Her pulse immediately became erratic and suddenly a flock of butterflies were zipping around in her stomach.

The sheriff cleared his throat. "There was a plastic bag on my desk when David was being processed." His eyes fixed on Emma. "I recall Deputy Hammond being extremely pissed—no pun intended—when he heard the toilet flush and realized the bag was gone."

She stared at his nameplate for a minute. *Kavanaugh*.

Offering Emma a sly grin, Sheriff Kavanaugh replaced his hat, brushing two fingers against the brim in a silent salute.

"See, we knew it was dope!" Hammond was insisting.

Regaining her composure, Emma turned back to the matter at hand. So the knight in shining armor from The Grill was the town sheriff. She couldn't allow that to distract her right now.

"Your Honor, without the actual contraband, or an analysis from a certified laboratory, the deputy can't really say what the defendant may or may not have possessed."

"She's right, Curtis."

"It was dope," Hammond repeated stubbornly.

Emma turned to the judge. "Respectfully, Your Honor, without any credible evidence to the contrary, the State can't prove my client had anything more innocuous than, say, oregano."

"It wasn't oregano," Hammond sneered. Small sweat globules formed on his upper lip. "It was a greenish brown plant substance. I know marijuana when I see it."

Emma smiled at the man's persistence. His attempt to camouflage his ineptitude with official-sounding rhetoric was admirable. Stupid, but admirable.

"I'd like a ruling on my motion for dismissal, Your Honor," Emma stated.

"Sorry, Hayden, Curtis. But the gal's got a point."

Blackwell twirled and returned to his chair at his counsel table. He wiped some perspiration from his brow with the back of his hand.

"Case dismissed," Judge Crandall ruled with an accompanying smack of his gavel.

David came out of his stunned silence when the bailiff came over to remove the shackles. "That's it?" he asked.

Nodding, Emma placed her hand on his forearm. "Yep. Unless you decide to do something else really dumb."

"No fine, no nothing?" David was incredulous.

"Nope."

"I can just go home?"

"You'll have to go back to the jail to fill out some paperwork," she explained. "Then you're free to go."

"Really?!"

"Yes," she promised him.

"You're really something, Miss McKinley," David said without so much as a trace of his former insolence.

"Yes, she is," came a male voice from behind her. "She certainly is something."

His hat was pulled low on his forehead, shielding his eyes and his expression from Emma. She didn't like that. Nor did she like the tauntingly curved smile on his chiseled mouth.

"Go on, David," she told her client.

"We haven't been properly introduced," the Sheriff said as soon as David was whisked off by the bailiff.

"You've told me your name," Emma replied coolly. "You did forget to mention your official title, *Sheriff*." She made the last word sound like a sarcastic expletive. Offering him her back, Emma stuffed her file into her briefcase, grabbed her purse, and headed toward the exit. It was blocked by six feet, four inches of Conner Kavanaugh.

Reluctantly, she lifted her eyes to his shadowed face.

He leaned forward. She could just feel the heat from his large body. "You know, if you make one of my deputies look like a total fool, it's like pointing the finger of blame right at me."

Giving him her brightest smile, Emma sweetly purred, "You're just mad because I got to choose the finger."

CHAPTER THREE

The state of Florida issued Emma a battered metal desk that tilted every time she leaned on the left edge. Needing to steady her work surface, she hiked up her skirt and got down on her hands and knees. She held a folded square of paper between her teeth. Using her shoulder for leverage, she forced the uneven leg off the floor and shoved the paper brace underneath. Then she promptly whacked her head on the base of the drawer.

"Damn!" she muttered.

"Miss McKinley?"

She was still rubbing the sore spot on the top of her head when she pushed herself off the floor. A woman, looking frail and uncertain, stood in the doorway. She appeared a bit older than Emma—late thirties, maybe—but the woman wore her years in the deep lines etched into what once probably had been a very pretty face. Now, however, she just looked whipped.

"I'm Emma McKinley," she said as she sat in her seat. "Please come in."

A thin cotton dress fell loosely from shoulders that were as limp and lifeless as the out-grown, dirty blond-dull brown hair she had pulled back into a barrette. Wisps of home-fashioned, uneven bangs hung on her small forehead, catching in clumps of blue mascara each time she blinked.

The woman moved quickly, in awkward motions that hinted at an underlying uneasiness. Once settled on the edge of one of the hideous green plaid chairs opposite Emma, the woman kept a death grip on her scuffed, vinyl handbag.

"I'm Jeanine Segan," she introduced herself.

One of Emma's brows arched when she connected the name.

"David is my son," she explained in a hurried rush of breath. "I just wanted to come here and thank you in person."

"I was just doing my job," Emma answered, holding the woman's gaze. The woman annoyed her. She should have been in court. "David could have used your support today."

Pain flashed in her eyes and she winced at the unmasked censure in Emma's tone. "I wanted to be there," Jeanine insisted. "It's just that Skeeter—well, he didn't want me to go."

"And Skeeter is?"

"I live with him," Jeanine answered, lowering her eyes. "I moved in with him when I lost my last job."

"And David?"

"I guess he's been staying with his friends. Anyways,

Skeeter says he's old enough to do for himself," she recited as if by rote.

"And what do you think?"

Her head came up slowly, her eyes glistening with unshed tears. "I think my son still needs his *maman*."

Emma was curious about the French dialect and the content of her statement. She regarded Jeanine for several seconds before asking, "Why don't you just tell…Skeeter to let your son live with you? Or better still, tell Skeeter to take a hike and raise your son?"

"Because I don't got nowheres else to go."

"Surely there are shelters, someplace you could get help."

Jeanine's expression grew cold and distant. "There are such places, Miss McKinley, but not here in Purdue. I was born here. I stay here."

With a man you clearly despise, who obviously doesn't give a damn about the welfare of your seventeen-year-old son, Emma thought angrily.

"I was a good mother," Jeanine continued. "I took good care of my son, 'specially when he was young. The Burkes let him have the run of the place."

Burke? The name sparked excitement in Emma's brain. That name had been mentioned in the news clippings. Struggling to keep her expression neutral, she asked, "You worked for Maddison Burke?"

"*Oui*," Jeanine said with a nod. "I cooked and cleaned for that family until—"

"Do you still cook and clean?"

Jeanine appeared confused. "*Pardon?*"

"Do you still cook and clean for hire?" Emma repeated, weaving her fingers together.

Jeanine's body seemed to sink into the chair. "Um… well…Mrs. Burke said I stole some money."

"Did you?"

"*Non!*" Jeanine insisted, twisting the handle of her purse. "But for a long time no one will hire me."

Emma made her decision in a flicker of a second. "I'm desperate to find a housekeeper. There's a small apartment on the top floor of my home. Two bedrooms, a bath, and a small kitchen."

"You want me to come to work for you?"

Ignoring her startled question, Emma continued. "You can have Wednesdays and Sundays off. I don't eat breakfast and I quite often miss dinner. The house is a mess because I still haven't finished unpacking."

"You're willing to give me a job? Just like that?"

"With two conditions."

She watched the budding light of excitement dim in the other woman's eyes.

"David comes with you. Skeeter doesn't. Is that acceptable?"

"I…um…"

"You'll receive a salary of five hundred dollars weekly plus free room and board."

Jeanine's expression grew suddenly wary. "That's twice what the Burkes paid me. Why you doing this?"

"I'm a practical woman, Mrs. Segan. I need a housekeeper. You need a job that allows you to support yourself and your child. David needs you if he's going to have a decent chance at life." *And I want information about the Burkes.*

Emma sensed vacillation in the other woman. "Is that acceptable?"

"I'm not sure Skeeter will let me go so easily. You see, I'm his…I sort of provide…"

"Not anymore," Emma told her. "You have two choices here. You can either put out for Skeeter and sit back while your son's life goes to hell in a handbasket. Or," Emma paused to stand. "You can take back your responsibility for your life and David's. The choice is yours."

"I'll think about it," Jeanine hedged.

Shrugging, Emma said, "Suit yourself, but I need an answer by Friday." Grabbing a pen, she scribbled her home address and cellphone number on the back of her business card.

Jeanine was hesitant as she took it, then she backed out of the room.

"I'll keep my fingers crossed," Emma whispered.

* * *

She didn't think about Jeanine Segan for the next three hours. She was too busy trying to digest the voluminous pile of work she'd inherited from her predecessor.

She was reading a police report on a case up for arraignment in the morning. Her client, Willis Maddox, was charged with indecent exposure and lewd and lascivious behavior, a fourth-degree sex offense. Reading the facts, she decided that Willis was obviously an emotionally disturbed man. He had twenty-plus years of history with the criminal justice system and almost all of the court interactions recommended assistance for his mental disability. Irritation welled inside her as she read the long list of priors and the related list of incarcerations. Of course, she thought, Willis had never received proper treatment. "And people wonder why guys like this reoffend," she grumbled softly.

The shrill ring of the telephone startled her. It also made her aware of the fact that it was late.

"Hello?"

"Emma? I've been calling you at home for hours."

Pulling her glasses off, Emma stretched in her chair. "Sorry, but you know how it is with a new job."

"Not that job," her sister scoffed. "I still can't believe you're in Purdue. I really think you've lost it this time."

"I know what I'm doing."

"No you don't," Amelia insisted. "What you're doing is dangerous."

"And working with the criminal element in New York wasn't?" Emma replied dryly.

"Come off it!" Amelia wailed through the receiver. "What do you think the good people of Purdue will do when they find out—"

"No one is going to find out," Emma assured her sister. "I don't plan on hanging around long after I get what I came here for."

"Mom isn't getting any better. In fact, each day she seems to be getting worse."

The update felt like a stab in the heart.

"They put her on a ventilator because of you."

"Amelia Rose," Emma warned, using her sister's full name for effect, "I need to do this before Mamma dies."

"You found something, didn't you?" Amelia asked. "You can't lie to me, Emma. I know you found something at Mamma's house that you didn't share with me. I can sense you're hiding something."

"Don't start that, Amelia. I'm really much too tired to argue the cosmic bond between identical twins with you again."

"I don't care."

Emma could see her sister's face, lower lip thrust out in a pout.

"I have a bad feeling about this, Emma. And this is just adding to my stress, what with the pressure from the doctors about Mamma."

"Is she suffering?" Emma asked.

"She's about the same. She's hooked up to about seven horrible machines." Amelia took an audible breath. "We need to end this, Emma. This isn't what Mamma wanted."

"Not yet," she answered with conviction, shoving her glasses back on. "Look, Amelia, I have a ton of stuff to get through. I'll call you this weekend." She didn't wait for her sister's farewell, she just hung up. "Note to self: get caller I.D."

* * *

Silently he stood in the shadows, watching her. The prim, professional jacket was gone. Her hands were behind her head. In the soft glow of the desk lamp, he could make out the curves of her body straining against her blouse. He felt an immediate and inappropriate heaviness in his groin.

She tugged gently at some pins, then that mane of blond hair tumbled down and framed her face, reflecting the light. With her hair down, she looked younger. More like when she was at The Grill. Seeing her in action at the courthouse had been impressive, to say the least. She had poise, grace, and enough self-confidence to fill a stadium.

The glasses, which would have looked frumpy on anyone else, somehow managed to make her seem even more sexy. He was wondering what it would be like to slip those glasses from her face and look into her eyes.

He found out. Emma McKinley removed her glasses then looked up and saw him standing in her doorway.

Conner grinned sheepishly, feeling a lot like he had when he was twelve, the day his mother had caught him in the swamp with Rayleen Doucet.

"Evening, counselor."

"A little late for appointments, Sheriff," she returned tightly.

"I brought you a beer," he said as he waltzed into her office. Ignoring her little snort, Conner fell into the chair across from her and plopped a cold six-pack on the desk. "You said you were partial to beer."

"I'm also partial to drinking alone."

"That's not good for you." Conner sighed as he took a bottle from the carton. Bracing the cap against the edge of the desk, he brought his hand down on the bottle, flipping its top. He brought the bottle to his lips and took a swallow, just to fend off the explosion of foam trying to escape. All the while, his eyes held hers.

With a definite challenge in his eyes, Conner carefully took the bottle away from his lips and offered it to her.

Her hesitation lasted about a nanosecond, then she accepted the beer. Her lips, which no longer shone with gloss as they had earlier in the day, parted as she raised the beer to her mouth. Her eyes never left his.

"How'd you know I was here?"

Conner opened a bottle for himself. "I figured you would have a lot to do." He shifted into the seat, crossing his legs pretty much to keep her from noticing that he was interested in more than just her intellect. "So, what happened at that high-powered New York firm you used to work for?"

Her eyes narrowed. "Where did you hear that?"

"Elgin said something to Judge Crandall, who said something to Wayne, the bailiff. Wayne told Sue, the clerk—"

"This is very fascinating," Emma interrupted him. "But I have no intention of sharing gossip with you."

"I don't engage in gossip. I just listen to it," He watched her stiffen at his attempted humor.

"Rumors can be dangerous things, Sheriff."

"Conner," he corrected. "My friends call me Conner."

"But we aren't friends," Emma pointed out.

"Are you always so prickly, or is it just me?"

"I'm not prickly. I am simply trying to politely let you know that I'm not interested in anything other than a professional, working relationship when the need arises."

"We played a little rock-paper-scissors-gun in the parking lot, but I don't recall having asked you out, Emma."

"Don't call me Emma."

"Why not?"

"Because only my friends call me Emma."

"My mamma was right," Conner sighed.

"Right about what?"

"She always said a good education ruins a good southern woman."

Her smile was breathtaking. It brought a sparkle to her eyes that warmed him in places he was trying to ignore.

"You have a nice smile, Emma. You ought to practice using it more often."

"I smile a lot," she told him.

It was the first time he had heard her voice without that edge. It was a soft, deep, feminine sound that was real pleasing on the ears.

"So." He took another swallow. "What did Jeanine want?"

Her smile faded and her expression closed tighter than the barred doors of his jail.

"How did you know Jeanine was here?"

"Do you always answer a question with a question?"

"When I don't understand the motivations of the person interrogating me."

Conner chuckled. "You are a suspicious little thing, aren't

you?" He raised his hand, silencing the lecture he sensed she was planning. "I take back the 'little thing' part."

"I offered Jeanine a job."

"Here?"

"No."

She took another drink of beer. His eyes followed the path of the drink, along the tapered smoothness of her throat.

"I need a housekeeper."

"So you hired Jeanine," he concluded. "You some sort of social worker?"

"You're the second person to ask me that today. And for the record, no, I am not a social worker. My motives are more selfish. I don't like to cook or clean."

"You really aren't much of a southern belle, are you, Emma?"

"Sorry to disappoint you."

Conner leaned forward and spoke in a provocatively low tone. "I don't think you could disappoint me, Emma."

"Don't do that," she told him, though her protest wasn't quite as fervent as it could have been.

"Do what?"

"Make insinuations."

He leaned back, taking a drink in hopes he could wash away some of the desire knotted in his stomach. He couldn't remember the last time he had wanted a woman on sight. He wondered why he wanted this one. She wasn't even close to his type. Babes with attitude were always more trouble than they were worth. And this one definitely had attitude.

"So, want to go to a party with me?"

Surprise registered on her face immediately. His invitation had definitely caught her off guard.

"Why would I want to do that?"

"To be neighborly," he suggested with a grin.

One of her pale brows lifted. "You seem to put a lot of emphasis on being neighborly."

"My mamma raised me with a true appreciation for southern hospitality. Didn't yours?"

He almost missed the tightening of her delicate fingers holding the bottle. He marveled at her control. He wondered why she kept such a short leash on her emotions. The notion of exploring this woman's personality was almost as appealing as the thought of exploring the blatant sensuality she seemed so hell-bent on hiding from the world.

"My family wasn't much on appearances."

"Very good," he said, raising his bottle in a pseudo salute. "Nice lawyerly non-answer."

Emma leveled her gaze on him. "Maybe that's why I am a lawyer."

"Good one, too."

He'd found it. This woman wasn't interested in his comments on her beauty. She hadn't exactly welcomed his half-hearted attempts at seductive banter. Complimenting her professional abilities brought a softness to her features and a relaxed smile to her mouth.

"Thank you."

"You made an ass out of Curtis Hammond." Conner laughed aloud, recalling the deputy's tirade back at the station following his disastrous court appearance. "He spent most of the day cursing you every way to Sunday."

"I'm sure he did."

"He'll probably try to get even with you."

"Really?"

Conner nodded. "I'm guessing you're in for more than your fair share of traffic tickets."

"I'll make a note," she groaned.

Her head tilted to one side and her hair caught the light as it fell across her shoulder. "I don't suppose you'd be willing to put in a good word for me?" Emma asked.

"Depends."

"On what?"

"On whether you go to the party with me."

"What kind of party is this?" she asked.

She didn't say no. That was good. That was very good. "It's something of a coming out party."

Her lips curved into a frown. "One of those southern debutante things? No thanks."

"The guest of honor is definitely southern, but I don't think she's hankering for debutante status."

"Good for her."

"No," Conner corrected. "Good for you."

"Me?" She blinked.

"It seems the town of Purdue is clamoring to get an up-close look at you. Especially after you humiliated Curtis and Hayden during your first hour on the job."

"Why would the town of Purdue care? I was just doing the job they're paying me to do."

"Okay, so maybe not the whole town," Conner relented. "But the movers and shakers wish to make your acquaintance."

Emma laughed. "And they sent you as their emissary?"

Conner saluted. "Sheriff and chief errand boy."

She cocked her head. "You don't impress me as the kind of man who would be anyone's errand boy."

"Maybe not. But I answer to the mayor and the town council." There was just enough truth in the statement to make it sound legit. At least he hoped so.

"So, when is this party?"

Conner checked his watch. "Starts in about fifteen minutes."

"Tonight?"

"Nine o'clock at Stella's."

"This is nuts," she scoffed. "I'm practically dead on my feet. And who or what is Stella's?"

"She owns the restaurant on Rawlings Street. Whenever there is something that needs discussing, it's discussed at Stella's."

"How quaint," she sighed. "Do I also vote and pay my water bill at Stella's?"

"If you want to," Conner answered. "So, what do you say? I'll run you by there; you can meet the most influential men in Purdue. Have some coffee and a slice of mud pie. I'll have you home by eleven."

"What about women?"

"I haven't been seeing anyone on a regular basis."

"Not you!" she groaned. "Your personal life is of no interest to me. I was simply asking if there are any influential women in Purdue?"

"Why?"

"Because I think having a female point of view in local matters is in keeping with the democratic principles of our society."

Conner grinned, leaning forward. "I agree. But what I was asking is why my personal life is of no interest to you?"

She was flustered. He could tell by the way her lashes fluttered before she lowered her eyes. "I was just letting you know our boundaries."

"I got that part. I'm just asking why we need boundaries before we actually get to know one another."

"What is it with you?" Hostility flashed in her eyes. "Do you think that just because you have a decent build and a relatively attractive face that all women should fall at your feet?"

"It has been known to happen," Conner teased. Her annoyance was amusing him. "But to answer your original question, there is one woman in Purdue with some pretty hefty influence."

"Who is that?"

"Renae Burke," Conner answered. "Her husband is Maddison Burke, Mayor of Purdue and soon-to-be announced candidate for the U.S. Senate. Renae is damned determined to get him there, too."

"Maddison Burke is running for the Senate?"

"You know Burke?" Conner asked.

"Just from history," she answered, though her voice was softer.

Sucking in a deep breath, holding it, then expelling it slowly, Conner stroked the shadow of stubble on his chin. "His greatest claim to fame may always be his association with the assassination of the president."

"Does he talk about it?"

"No! No one in Purdue ever talks about it. Most folks are happy to forget that the President and our governor were gunned down within the city limits."

"But that was more than twenty years ago."

"It's still an open wound," Conner explained. "On the anniversary of the assassinations Purdue always gets a sound bite and an unpleasant reminder of our infamy. We'd prefer to be known for our great oranges and cane sugar."

"We don't always get what we want."

He wasn't sure if it was the philosophical lilt of her voice, or simply that her posture was less combative. At any rate, he detected a definite change in the woman seated behind the desk.

"So, are you game to give the good people of Purdue a few minutes of your time? Or are you going to send me back empty-handed?"

Retrieving her jacket from the back of her chair, Emma stood and said, "Sure, but a very, very few minutes."

"Good, Hayden would have been really pissed if you'd have slammed him twice in the same day." He rose from his seat and followed her out of the office.

"Hayden Blackwell?" she asked as she pulled the door closed behind them.

"He's on the town council in addition to being our reigning D.A."

"And Judge Crandall?"

Conner smiled and placed a hand at the small of her back. His smile widened when he felt the soft curve of her spine beneath his touch. "He's the head of the town council."

"Quaint," he heard her mumble as they took the elevator to the first floor.

"Then there's Wayne."

"The bailiff?"

"By day," Conner explained. "On the second Tuesday of every month he's the Council Secretary."

"Incestuous little town you have here, Sheriff."

"We try."

* * *

Stella's turned out to be a glorified coffee shop. The front façade was a picture window with the daily specials painted in bright turquoise lettering. There was a smaller sign hanging from the knob that read, CLOSED FOR A PRIVATE PARTY AT NINE O'CLOCK.

Emma thought the placed smelled a lot like the courthouse—coffee, cigarettes, and bacon, all stale.

Animated conversations stopped abruptly as they entered, only adding fuel to the fire of anticipation burning in her stomach. Still, Emma was able to muster enough confidence to meet the dozen or so pairs of curious eyes pointed in her direction.

"Nice work, Sheriff," Judge Crandall said. "So glad you could drop by, Miss McKinley."

Crandall offered a personable smile along with the hand he held out in her direction. She smelled the faint scent of woodsy cologne and wished she would have taken time to freshen her appearance. In a rare display of self-consciousness, Emma smoothed her hair with her fingers.

"Nice to see you again, Your Honor."

"I was quite impressed with your skills, young lady."

"Thank you." Emma felt a strange heat on her back. It took a few seconds for her to decipher the cause. It was Conner Kavanaugh. The man was behind her, to the left, his hand resting just at the slope of her hip. She could feel the strength in his hand and her mind flashed an instant image of sculpted muscle and broad shoulders.

"Miss McKinley, I'm Maddison Burke."

"Mr. Mayor." She greeted the man with polite coolness.

He preened at her recognition as his dark eyes roamed over her face. Emma held her breath, scared that he might recognize her, sadistically hoping that he would.

"I can see Kavanaugh filled you in," the mayor said.

"Yes," she murmured. "The sheriff certainly doesn't seem to suffer from shyness." She discreetly shoved his hand off her hip.

Maddison crooked his elbow in invitation, and Emma let him lead her to a semicircle of expectant faces. Emma was amazed. They seemed to all be dressed alike. Like a Stepford

Wife Town Council. Or like the uniforms she'd been forced to endure during her tenure at the St. Francis Academy.

Maddison dipped his salt and pepper head with each introduction. His square-tipped fingers never left her arm. "—is Kenny Simms."

"Mr. Simms," Emma repeated, adding his name to the mental tally in her head. Simms, transparent red hair, sour expression, didn't offer his hand.

"Miss," he managed, though she got the impression that even that civility grated on the stumpy little man. One of the things that made her a good attorney was her ability to read people. Simms's dislike was duly noted as she moved on to the next introduction.

When he was finished, Maddison asked, "So what do you think of our little town council here, Miss McKinley?"

"Very nice," she evaded. "I'm still confused as to why I was summoned here this evening."

Maddison's eyebrows arched exaggeratedly. "Summoned?" he parroted, adjusting the knot in his designer tie. "Why, we were just anxious to get to meet you. Heard you made quite an impression on Judge Crandall today."

"I was only doing what Purdue hired me to do."

Maddison's smile looked pained…no…forced. "And your efforts resulted in a young drug dealer getting off to sell more drugs in my town."

"The system did that, Mr. Mayor, not me."

Maddison gave her a patronizing look. "If you're as good as I hear, we can expect our jail to be empty come November."

"Election time?" Emma asked, careful to keep the derision out of her tone.

"I see you are very well informed."

It wasn't a compliment. That was evident by the narrowing of his eyes and the slight increase of pressure on her arm.

"I try to keep pace."

"Maddison, dear?" A cultured female voice wafted above the small crowd.

Emma turned and watched as a billow of beige silk floated in her direction. The woman's appearance screamed money and social breeding. It was everywhere—from the elegant arrangement of the soft hair twisted into a full chignon, to the tips of Italian leather pumps that perfectly matched her winter-white slacks.

"Evening, dear," the mayor said as he placed a kiss on the cheek she presented.

Emma smiled and tasted the vapor trail of the other woman's perfume. Clear, green eyes regarded her as the woman placed a heavily jeweled hand against the side of Maddison's face.

She disengaged herself from her husband and took a step toward Emma. "I'm Renae Burke," she announced, bending her wrist as she extended it.

Emma wasn't about to kiss her ring. She was amazed that Renae didn't look more than a minute older than she had at the time of the assassination.

"Emma McKinley."

Renae's smile was remote and reserved. "I'm so glad I was able to drop in while you were here."

Something told Emma this wasn't an accidental encounter. She would bet every last penny of her settlement that Renae Burke didn't rely on accidents.

"I was having dinner with a friend and managed to slip away just in the nick of time."

A bottle of beer appeared in Emma's hand. The mayor's wife glanced down at it with open disdain.

"Emma is partial to beer," Conner explained.

There was something way too familiar in the way he had said that. Emma felt her ire begin to rise.

"Ms. McKinley," she corrected in a loud whisper. "And I'm not particularly thirsty right now." She shoved the beer into the general vicinity of his chest. Her annoyance grew when he refused to take it. Instead, Conner just stood there with her knuckles against his rock-solid body.

Quelling the urge to yank open his waistband and pour the cold beer down his pants, Emma pulled her arm back.

"You about ready to head out?" Conner asked.

Renae and Maddison shared startled expressions. Renae spoke up. "You can't leave so early, dear."

"I'm sorry. I know it is early, but I've had a long day and tomorrow promises to be just as long."

"I told you we should have planned something for the weekend," Renae scolded her husband.

"We still can," Maddison gave Emma an expectant look. "If you're free on Saturday, perhaps we can put together a little something out at our home."

"I'll have to check my calendar," Emma replied sweetly. She swallowed her smile when she heard the offended catch of air from Renae. It was apparent that the First Lady of Purdue wasn't accustomed to being told 'perhaps'. So what? "It was a pleasure to meet you both."

A few minutes later Conner said, "That wasn't exactly the way to make friends in high places."

He held the door for her as she climbed into his SUV. "You're assuming I want friends in high places," she countered.

He got into the car and started the engine. "Renae Burke is a powerful, willful woman," he warned.

Emma angled herself in the seat and looked at his profile. She had to admit he was attractive in an appealingly rugged sort of way.

"You sound like you don't care much for the mayor's wife."

The fabric of his khaki shirt drew taut against his chest when he shrugged. Emma could easily make out the washboard-tight muscle of his flat stomach. She looked away, not wanting her mind to go down that path. Not now. Maybe not ever.

"She keeps Maddison in line."

"Does he need it?"

"Sometimes," Conner admitted with a wry smile. "He's got the ambition, but Renae has most of the smarts. Maddison's mostly drive and ego." Conner stopped for a red light next to her office, then turned and asked, "Sure you have to get right home?"

Emma breathed in irritation. "I am not interested, Sheriff."

His eyes flashed with sudden realization. "Are you…I mean, you do like men, right?"

Emma couldn't stop the laughter. "I get it. Any woman not interested in you must be a lesbian, right? And you said *Maddison* had an ego. Thanks for an interesting evening." Emma jumped from the SUV and hustled to her car. Conner didn't get the last word, but he did get the last sound. His tires squealed as he pulled out into traffic.

* * *

The house she had bought on an earlier trip to Purdue was set back from the main road. The driveway was guarded by massive live oaks dripping with Spanish moss. A string of muttered curses eased out of her as she made her way down the drive. "Note to self: leave a light on," she grumbled in the thick and unfamiliar blackness.

A bell chimed when she left the car door open in order to retrieve mail from the box. "Damn it!" she cried, bringing her cut knuckle to her lips. She made two more notes to herself—replace the mailbox and update tetanus shot.

She parked in front of her house. Shadows of pale moonlight danced across the porch as she cautiously navigated each step. With the assortment of mail tucked under her arm, Emma was about to put her key in the lock when she felt something beneath her foot.

Opening the door, she ferreted out the light switch just inside and to the left. Still unsure of which switch controlled what, she flipped all three switches. Yellowish light spilled from every direction. It took her eyes a few seconds to adjust as she tossed the mail in on the foyer table then went back out to retrieve whatever she had stepped on in the darkness.

Reaching down, she scraped a smashed white lily off the wooden planks and lifted it into the light.

The petals were limp and partially dislodged from the bud. The stem felt warm and sticky. It was fractured in several places from where she had stepped on it. But that wasn't the disturbing aspect of the single blossom.

Emma looked at her palm, feeling panic well inside her. She let out a scream when she realized what she was holding.

The warm stickiness from the stem had stained her hand with blood.

CHAPTER FOUR

Bloody blossom in hand, she quickly went inside, bolting the door on the way. She wasn't normally fearful of being alone, but then again, she'd never been sent a bloody flower before. She made another mental note to have an alarm system with motion detectors and video installed ASAP.

Her list of suspects was long. It could have been a member of the town council, though that they would get to her place before she did seemed unlikely; the blood was still fresh. So her second, and most likely, suspect was Skeeter. Assuming Jeanine had told him about the job offer, he'd sounded like the kind of guy who'd pull off something so juvenile. If Skeeter was going to be a problem, better to nip it in the bud—no pun intended—now rather than later. She was pissed. The last thing she needed was some looney ex-boyfriend creeping around. Time to let the sheriff do his job. Her housekeeper might be afraid of Skeeter but she sure as hell wasn't. After New York, there was no way she was going to let someone else dictate any aspect of her life.

She pulled out her cell and dialed 9-1-1.

"What is your emergency?" an operator asked in a calm tone.

"This is Emma McKinley. I need the sheriff at 4315 Carlyle Drive."

"For what purpose?"

"I've been threatened."

"I'll send a deputy out now."

"I don't want a deputy," Emma argued. "I want the sheriff. He knows me." *Or thinks he does.* That part didn't matter. She wanted to skip the underlings and go straight to the top. In the long run, she figured it would be more expedient. Conner may be hitting on her but she could and would use that to her advantage.

"Hold the line please."

She came back on in a nano-second. "Sheriff Kavanaugh is on his way. Do you need to stay on the line with me until he arrives?"

"No, thank you."

As she was hanging up the phone she heard the sound of sirens in the distance. But as they grew closer, Emma started to question the intelligence of calling the sheriff for help. After all, the flower could just be a prank. Then she'd look like a fool. For some reason she wasn't yet ready to acknowledge, she didn't want him thinking of her as foolish.

By the time he pulled his SUV behind her car in the driveway, she had calmed her nerves.

The SUV arrived in a spray of gravel and Conner got

out in a single, agile motion, unholstering his gun as he approached.

"Put that away," Emma chastised him. "Who are you going to shoot? Me?"

He smiled. "The thought did cross my mind. Dispatch said she had a frantic woman on the line demanding my presence. Did she get the address wrong?"

He stepped up onto the porch. She pointed to the drying blood on her brand new welcome mat. "I came home and found a lily soaked in blood on my porch."

"Well, you aren't exactly getting a reputation for your friendliness," he said as he knelt by the stained rug. "Sure looks like blood," he concluded.

"Gee, ya think?"

He stood, forcing her to crane her neck to look into his clear gray eyes rimmed in dark lashes. "Do you have the flower?"

"In here," she said, leading him inside her house. It had an open floorplan and, save for a pile of boxes, a sofa, loveseat, coffee table and chair—nothing else. She was waiting on another delivery from Tampa scheduled for late the next afternoon. She pointed to the sink.

Conner took out a latex glove and folded it in his hand so he could grab the stem without putting the glove on his hand.

And it was a large hand, Emma noted. For a scant second she wondered what it might feel like to have that hand run along the side of her body. Feel his fingers splayed in her hair.

Stop it!

"Probably just kids," he opined. "This place has been empty for nearly two years and the kids used it like a fort until it got sold to you."

"Oh. No one told me that."

He shot her a charming smile that made her weak in the knees. "Just like no one told you you way overpaid for the place?"

"How do you know what I paid?" she demanded, her ire returned with a vengeance.

"Your realtor told my clerk and—"

"Your clerk told you," she finished his sentence. "I don't think I like Purdue very much," she grumbled.

"Maybe this will change your mind. You got some blood on you," Conner said. He took a towel from the roll by the sink and gently wiped her cheek. His touch was as soft as a whisper and in sharp contrast to the heat of his warm breath against her face.

Say something pithy. Something. Anything! God, she hated feeling vulnerable. It was an unfamiliar and unwelcome emotion.

Instead she just stared up at him as he let the towel fall away and cupped her chin in his palm. His thumb made several circles on her skin then moved higher, brushing against her open lower lip until she was afraid a moan would escape. Her heart skipped several beats and her mind spun, *Damn it.* One touch and she was jelly? This man was going to be trouble.

"I'll fill out a report," he said in a steady voice.

Emma just nodded like some besotted fool. But she used the time he was in his truck to gather her scattered wits. How on earth could this man's touch be more erotic than a kiss from anyone else?

She supposed it was when that man was Conner Kavanaugh.

CHAPTER FIVE

After a fitful night dreaming about a tall man with dark hair and clear, gray eyes, Emma rolled off the uncomfortable air mattress and headed downstairs.

There were three items on her countertop: her beloved Keurig, her purse, and her phone, plugged into its charger. The refrigerator was equally sparsely populated, with only a container of cream and a carton of leftover Chinese food inside.

The sun was just peeking over the horizon as she took her speed-made cup of coffee into the living room and sat on the sofa. From her vantage point, she could see one-hundred-eighty degrees of lake view. The lake was two miles wide and nine miles long. There was a dock out back of her home but currently, it was occupied. By a really big alligator. She shivered automatically. The lake was nice to look at but only from inside the safety and comfort of her home.

Which would feel more like a home when the rest of her

furniture arrived. She was excited about that, actually. After years of living with roommates or in a furnished apartment, this was her first real home. Her first attempt to decorate. It was exciting yet daunting.

She was startled by the shrill ring of her cell phone. Placing her mug on the coffee table, she raced into the kitchen and yanked out the power cord. "Hello?"

"Miss McKinley?"

"Jeanine?" she asked, fairly sure she recognized the voice even though it was barely above a whisper.

"I'd like the job. If it's still available."

"It's yours," Emma said. "When can you start?" The sooner, the better. "I've got some deliveries scheduled for today so having you in the house would be a Godsend.""

"Can we come now? David and me?"

"Sure. Maybe later David could look into going back to school."

"I was hoping you could talk to him about that."

Emma checked the clock on the microwave. "Can you be here in an hour?"

"Yes ma'am."

"You don't have to 'ma'am' me, Jeanine. Emma is fine."

"Thank you, Miss Emma."

She got off the phone and raced upstairs for a shower. She'd correct Jeanine's use of "Miss" when they arrived.

She dried her hair and applied her make-up, then put on a pretty pink shift dress and grabbed a white sweater that she draped over one bent arm before she slipped into a pair of ballet flats. Like most things she did, the outfit was intentional. Today's case—assuming Bill's kid still had chicken pox—called for a younger, less aggressive woman. Her client was six-six. If she didn't seem frightened of him, then neither would judge and/or jury.

She was halfway down the staircase when the doorbell rang. "Hi," Emma said as she opened the door wide. Her smile faltered when she saw Jeanine was sporting a purplish eye that was nearly swollen shut. "Jesus Christ," she muttered as she took the small suitcase from the woman. "Skeeter?"

Jeanine nodded.

"He's a total dick," David added as he carried a box inside that seemed very heavy based on his body language. "Where do you want me to put my stuff?" he asked.

"Up two flights, then pick a room. They're both about the same size."

Emma led Jeanine to the living room. "Do you need to go to the hospital?"

Jeanine shook her head. "It'll be fine in a day or two."

"How about a cup of coffee?"

Jeanine smiled and winced simultaneously. "That would be wonderful."

"Black?"

"Cream if you have it."

Emma brewed Jeanine's coffee and then another for herself. She carried them back into the living room just as David was coming down the stairs. "Want some?" Emma asked.

"Sure. I've got two more boxes in the car."

"Not a problem; just shout when you're ready." Emma

watched as he walked out on the deck and down to what she generously called a car. It was some sort of 1980s compact with one door painted with primer; there was red tissue paper covering a broken tail light; and the antenna looked as if part of it had been snapped off. The car was jerry-rigged with a trailer-sort of thing that carted a small, sad-on-the-eyes motorcycle.

She could take care of that later; for now, she delivered Jeanine's coffee.

"Thank you, Miss Emma."

She smiled at the battered woman. "No 'Miss,' okay? Emma is just fine."

"'kay. I can't thank you enough for all this," Jeanine gushed. "Last night was real ugly. I knew you were right and I had to get away from Skeeter."

No shit. But I don't want to talk about Skeeter, I'm far more interested in Renae Burke and her merry band of friends.

* * *

Today was a huge day and Conner was determined to make it special. In preparation, he'd painted the guestroom bright pink with purple accents. He'd found a girly bedspread that was also pink with big purple polka dots, and it fit perfectly on the white four-poster bed he'd bought along with a matching end table and dresser. With the help of the sales lady, he'd gotten some throw pillows and at the toy store he'd found a stuffed purple elephant.

Samantha loved elephants. Conner smiled at the finished

room and then closed the door. He wanted to see his daughter's expression when she opened it and found he'd done so much in honor of her first visitation since his ex had moved to Chicago.

He checked his watch again. Time was creeping by. Sam's plane didn't land for another two hours but he was all set and ready to walk out the door. Maybe he could kill some time at Stella's having coffee before he made the fifty-five-mile trek to the airport to greet his only child.

He didn't really need more coffee. He was already full of nervous energy. Though they spoke on the phone a couple of times a week, it wasn't the same as actually being with her. As he drove into town he silently cursed the family court judge who had allowed his ex to move their daughter out of state. The judge had determined that his ex and her new husband had the more stable environment, just because Conner was on call at all times. It didn't hurt that Lisa's new husband had more money than God while Conner had had to take out a second mortgage on his house and all he'd received in return was a shitty visitation schedule.

Samantha was smart and with a little pull from her stepfather, she'd gotten into a prestigious math and technology school. This meant she had quarters instead of semesters, and Samantha had decided to spend her spring quarter with Conner. He arrived at Stella's with more than forty-five minutes to kill.

* * *

Emma followed a deputy to a holding cell adjacent to the courtrooms. She had learned to ignore the catcalls of prisoners years ago. Her client was in the next to last cell. He was wearing an orange jumpsuit and shower shoes. Not the best choice for a bond hearing, but it was what it was.

"Mr. Willis Maddox?" she asked, referring to one of the forms she'd pulled from her briefcase.

A very large man with a dark completion and even darker eyes turned and gave her a once-over. "Yeah. Who're you?"

"I'm Emma McKinley from the Public Defender's Office. I'll be your attorney today."

His brows scrunched together. "What happened to Mr. Bill?"

"He has a sick child," she answered. "Can you tell me in your own words what happened leading to your arrest?"

"I was washing my clothes and that jerk-off deputy said I was naked in public, so he arrested me."

"Was it Deputy Hammond?" she asked.

Willis shook his head. "The young one. Deputy Littleton."

"Why were you washing your clothes in public?" Emma asked.

"'Cause that's where I live," he explained. "Got myself a fine little place down by the creek."

"Do you always wash clothing naked?"

Willis' head tilted and he looked at her as if to say *idiot*. "I ain't got but one pair of clothes, lady."

"Okay," Emma said as she scribbled a note on the file. "Anything else I should know?"

He shook his head. "I just hope my things are still there when I get back."

"Things?"

"Got me some canned food and a camp light and my tent, 'course. Good pickings for some."

"Where *exactly* is *there*?" she asked.

"Creek about thirty yards through the woods at the east end of Presidential Memorial Park."

Emma's mind wandered when she processed the name that had defined her whole life. If anyone figured out who she was, they'd probably run her out of town in a New York minute—everyone except the person who'd been sending her old news clippings of the assassination for the last six weeks. They'd started arriving just after her mother's first stroke. Then seemingly out of the blue she'd received a call from a former professor abut a job opening in Purdue. It struck Emma as too coincidental to be anything less than someone wanting her here for a reason. Fine. She wanted answers, too.

"Miss?" The bailiff arrived and unlocked the cell.

Maddox shuffled and his shackles rattled as he was escorted into the courtroom. Emma was right behind him. She placed her briefcase on the floor next to the defendant's table, retrieving her sweater and slipping it on.

Again, the weather in Purdue wasn't like the postcard version of Florida. It was spring in north Florida, and temperatures in the mornings hovered around sixty. It wasn't until afternoon that they warmed to the mid-seventies. However, here in the courtroom the air conditioning was set for the afternoon heat, making the room frigid this early in the morning.

She was keenly aware of her client's massive size. How could she not be? He was more than a foot taller than she was and a lot of solid muscle. "Stop grimacing," she whispered. "And let me do all the talking."

Judge Crandall entered from his antechamber and the bailiff called court into session. Hayden Blackwell was again seated at the State's Attorney's table. He offered her a weak smile before the judge said, "Call the first case."

"State versus Willis Maddox, Your Honor."

Judge Crandall looked at her. "Miss McKinley, how does your client plead?"

"Your Honor, my client moves for an immediate dismissal of all charges."

Hayden Blackwell's neck got red as he stood. "The defendant was found naked in public, Your Honor. If that isn't lewd and lascivious I don't know what is."

Emma cleared her throat and took a slip of paper out of her briefcase. "Your honor, at the time my client was washing his clothing, he was thirty yards deep in the woods. The statute clearly states under Section 7.01(a) '…the behavior must offend the sensibilities of those around the actor.' Were Deputy Littleton's sensibilities offended?"

"Let's ask him."

"Deputy Littleton, please take the stand."

A muscular, red-haired young man in full uniform came up and was sworn before taking his seat. The judge swiveled in his seat and asked, "Well, son. Were you offended?"

He shrugged. "It was dark and he's a big son of a bitch-man."

"May I inquire?" Emma asked.

"Your motion."

"Deputy Littleton. Were you offended by his size or the fact that he was naked?"

"Both."

Emma nodded. "Okay. I notice you're quite fit. Do you belong to a gym?"

"Yes, ma'am."

"Work out regularly?"

"Yes, ma'am."

"Shower after your workouts?"

His eyes narrowed on her like a couple of laser lights. "Yes."

"So you've seen your fair share of naked men, correct?"

"Correct."

"Then logically speaking it had to be my client's size and not his state of undress that offended you?"

"I guess."

Emma looked up to see the judge battling laughter. "Your Honor, I again move that this case be dismissed."

Blackwell was beet red and on his feet. "Save it, Hayden," the judge said. "Motion granted. The defendant is released herewith."

* * *

Conner was as close to the flight arrival area as TSA would allow. Even flashing his badge didn't get them to relax their rules. Luckily he was tall and could see clearly and he scanned the parade of passengers looking for his baby girl.

After what felt like a year had passed, he spotted her walking slowly up the terminal. She was wearing her pajamas. He silently cursed his ex for allowing her to travel like that.

"Sami!" he called as he waved his hand.

Nothing.

He tried again and still nothing. It wasn't until he positioned himself in front of her and she nearly barreled into him that she looked up from the cell phone in her hands. She offered him a bright smile and got up on tiptoes to kiss his cheek.

Conner wrapped his arms around her and drank in the smell of her hair. He patted the top of her head as she stepped out of his grasp. Only then did she pull twin earbuds out of her ears. "You on some sort of covert operation?" he asked.

She held them out for him. "These are my earbuds, Dad. No more wires."

"I'm still trying to master my DVR," he admitted.

"Dinosaur," she teased as she wound her arm through his. "I kinda brought a lot with me but Barry said he'll pay for the luggage overages."

"I think I can handle that without Barry."

"Let's go to baggage claim." They followed a red line painted on the floor to the only carousel in the small airport. "What am I looking for?" he asked.

Nothing.

"Sami?!" he said more firmly.

"What? Sorry, I was texting."

"I haven't seen you in six months and you're texting six minutes after you arrive?"

"Dad, I have friends."

"Do you have clothes?"

"What?"

He pointed in the general direction of her outfit. "Those look like P.J.s."

"Pajama pants are comfy and technically, these are lounge wear. So is my top. I didn't want to be cold or uncomfortable on the plane. Can we get some coffee?"

"Coffee? When did that start?"

She rolled her eyes. "I had to get up at o'dark-thirty to catch my flight. Oh wait! Those two plaid ones are mine."

Conner wrestled the bags off the carousel. "Did you pack rocks?"

"No," she said defensively. "Can we *please* get coffee on the way to your place?"

"Yes. But you really shouldn't drink that crap. Tears up your stomach."

She wasn't listening. She was back to texting.

Like some sort of pack mule, Conner dragged her luggage to his truck and lifted them—with some effort—into the back of the SUV.

"I hate riding around in a police car. It makes me look like a criminal," she whined.

Conner looked at her and smiled. "You're too pretty to be a criminal, Sami."

"Sam."

"Excuse me?"

"I don't go by Sami anymore. Just Sam."

"Okay. There's a 7-Eleven up ahead. I'll get you a cup of—"

"Ewww. No, Dad, like real coffee. You know, from a real barista?"

"Sorry," he said on an expelled breath. He'd have to go one town over to the coffee shop. It was a quaint place he'd been to once. Yeah, *once* he'd paid eight bucks for a cup of coffee.

They got out of the car and Sam said, "Smell that?"

"Yes."

"I love the smell of coffee brewing. And I know just what I want." Sam marched right up to the counter. Easy to do, because all of the other patrons were on computers or tablets with their pricey beverages within reach.

Sam smiled at the clerk and Conner was proud of his daughter's manners. In six months she'd gotten about three inches taller. She was a stunning girl with jet black hair well past her shoulders and beautiful blue eyes. Her outfit might be comfortable but it was formless, which was fine with him. She was sixteen, but he wasn't ready for her to grow up yet.

"I'd like a skinny frap with a half shot of vanilla and a half shot of hazelnut no whip. Dad?"

"Nothing for me," he said, then he paid the bill.

He let Sami—er, Sam—pick the table. Her behind barely hit the seat and she was already spinning her thumbs across her cell phone.

"Are we going to talk?" Conner asked, making sure he didn't sound annoyed even though he was.

"Hang on," she said. Then a few seconds later she looked up at him. "What?"

"Do we need to put some limits on that thing?" he asked, nodding at the state-of-the-art phone.

She looked horrified. "Never. I'd just die without my phone. It's my lifeline."

"Do you know how many perverts use social media to troll for victims?"

Again with the rolling eyes. "I'm only chatting with friends," she insisted. "People from school and all."

"If they're in school, why are they texting?"

"Because school is boring," she said the phrase as if it was etched on some plaque somewhere.

The barista called Sam's name and she went to retrieve her drink. "Ready?" she asked when she returned.

"Don't you want to sit down and enjoy that?"

"I got it to go," she said as she took a first cautious sip. "Mmmmm, good!"

"Home we go," he said.

The fifty-five-mile drive didn't turn out as he had hoped. Getting and holding his daughter's attention proved to be a challenge. She was either drinking her coffee or obliviously working the phone. Still, the closer they got to the house, the more excited Conner became. He knew she was going to be impressed with what he'd done. During her last visit the only thing he'd had in that room was a camping cot and a lamp. Now it was all about her.

They pulled into the driveway of the modest home Conner had bought the year after his divorce. It was nothing like the McMansion she lived in with Barry and his ex, but it was home.

Again he struggled to lug her bags out of the back of the truck, but this time Sam helped by rolling one of them up the stone walk to the front door. Inside, he paused at the alarm pad to enter the disarm code, then rolled the luggage toward the back hallway. "Here," he said as he stopped. "You go first."

Abandoning the bag, she walked around him and went to the closed door. She turned the knob and he asked, "What do you think?"

"I think a bottle of Pepto Bismol vomited in here."

CHAPTER SIX

Emma returned to the office with Willis Maddox in tow. His presence didn't go unnoticed. She had him sit in her office while she went to see her boss.

Elgin's secretary, Jenny, an attractive black woman in her late forties, showed her into Elgin Hale's office. Hale wasn't alone. Seated in one of the chairs across from his desk was a short, compact man in his mid-thirties who got to his feet and offered his hand. "Bill Whitley," he said, pumping her hand. "You must be my pinch hitter."

By his jerky movements and the sweat on his upper lip he seemed flustered, or nervous, or—hell, she had no idea; maybe he was about to have a damned heart attack. His hand was a bit clammy and she gave him a sympathetic smile as she released it, politely not wiping her damp fingers on her slacks. Even though Hale hadn't offered her a seat, she sat down in the visitor's chair anyway. "Nice to meet you. How's your…?"

"Son," he supplied. "No more fever but my wife has gotten someone to cover her shifts for the rest of the week. She's a nurse."

Handy. "I hope he recovers quickly."

"Thanks."

"Heard you took in a boarder," Elgin chimed in.

Emma smiled. "I *hired* a housekeeper. How did you know?"

"Skeeter told the guy who mows my lawn and—"

With a rueful shake of her head, Emma held up her hand. "I get it."

"Also hear you didn't come back from court alone."

She expelled a breath. Holy shit. Small towns. Everybody knew everybody's business almost before it happened. "Our client is indigent."

"So call Social Services." Hale leaned back in his seat and rubbed his bald head. "They're on a first name basis with Maddox."

"Willis Maddox?" Bill Whitley scoffed. "He's a career criminal."

She fixed her eyes on her colleague. "I read his rap sheet. No violence; almost everything is a simple trespass or a harmless misdemeanor. He just needs a little help."

Whitley rolled his eyes. "God save me, a true believer," he moaned.

Emma's spine stiffened. "Is there something wrong with that?"

"You're setting yourself up for disappointment," Bill warned.

"Rather disappointed than complacent."

"You won't get far if you're going to be a bleeding heart around here, honey. By the way, congratulations on being two for two," he told her, sounding far from complimentary.

Asshole. "Thank you." Emma kept her tone snark-free. "I just wanted to ask if it would be possible for me to take the rest of the day. I have furniture being delivered and I haven't settled into my house and—"

"Of course." Elgin nodded as he spoke. "See you first thing in the morning for the staff meeting."

"Staff meeting?"

"I thought someone would have told you," Elgin said. "Seven a.m. every Wednesday. Miss it and you're guaranteed to get all the crap cases."

"I'll be here," she promised before offering a tight farewell to Whitley. She made her way back to her small office.

Maddox stood when she entered, but Emma waved him back into his seat. "Give me a minute to organize myself and we can be on our way."

He did as told but she felt his gaze follow her around the room, suspicion glinting in his dark eyes. She was still a tad pissed at Whitley for treating her like some naive fool. Then again, he didn't know what she knew: that a trial shines light on the truth, even if that truth is ugly. And she wasn't in any condition to lecture him, not unless she was prepared to tell him her secret.

And that wasn't going to happen.

After completing some paperwork, Emma shut down her

laptop and tucked it inside her briefcase. "Ready?" she asked Maddox.

He nodded. "Yes, ma'am."

Emma said good-bye to her small office, stopping only to tell the receptionist that she could be reached on her cellphone for the rest of the day. Emma checked her watch. It was just after eleven. "Karen?" she asked the receptionist. "Is there a same-day furniture store around here?"

Karen gave her the name and directions for the furniture store as well as the closest Target. Maddox followed her to her Lexus, looking at the car like it was an alien spaceship. "Get in," Emma instructed.

Maddox folded his large frame into the passenger's seat. Once she was behind the wheel, Emma explained her plan. Reaching into her wallet, she took out a hundred dollars and said, "This is for food and clothing. I'm taking you to the Salvation Army. You can sleep there and get some more clothing at their store. I want you at my house tomorrow morning at six a.m., understood?"

"I don't need no handout," he said with a defiant lift of his chin.

"Good, because this isn't a handout, it's an advance on your salary." She thrust the money closer. "But if you buy so much as a can of beer with this the deal's off and you're on your own. Understand?"

"Yeah. What kinda work I gotta do for a hundred a week?"

"Everything," Emma answered. "I need a handyman. Someone I can trust. Someone who can help maintain my house and the grounds. The lawn is in desperate need of mowing. And I'll pay you an additional three hundred for the work once it is finished."

Maddox nodded. "I can spruce the place up real nice."

"I know you can," Emma agreed. "You'll also be getting meals, so all you really need to think about is finding some-place more appropriate to sleep."

"I like it outdoors," he insisted.

"Unless you like getting arrested for trespassing again, I suggest you learn to like the outside during normal park hours."

After giving him her home address, she dropped Maddox off at the Salvation Army then headed to the furniture store. She needed a little magic. And she needed it delivered today.

Furniture Barn was a huge warehouse-type building with a massive parking lot and one of those giant orange balloon people swaying on the roof holding a sign that read SALE. Money wasn't as much an issue as immediate delivery. She wasn't going to buy anything super expensive, but she had to furnish Jeanine and David's rooms or they'd spend their first night in her home sleeping on the hardwood floor.

As soon as she entered the building she was greeted by a perky saleswoman and the scent of leather.

"I'm Kiki," the woman introduced herself.

"Emma," she returned with a smile.

"What are we looking for today, Emma?"

"I need two bedroom suites and a kitchen table and chairs and I need them delivered today."

Kiki's green eyes lit up. "Follow me," she said. "Do you have any particular style in mind?"

"Something appropriate for a young man for one room." She thought back to when David was carrying in boxes. "And I'll need some sort of computer desk to go with that bedroom set. The second bedroom—well, I don't have a clue. Something white, maybe?"

"What size beds are you wanting?"

Emma did a little mental calculation. "Nothing bigger than a queen."

In spite of her pole dancer name, Kiki was very good at her job. She put together an ultra-modern suite for David's room and a pretty craftsman style room for Jeanine. Then Emma selected lamps and area rugs and two small flat screens just in case they wanted to watch television. The up-stairs apartment had a small kitchen, so on Kiki's advice she picked a tall butcher block table with four backed stools.

In a little over an hour, Emma was signing the credit card pad and taking her receipt with the guaranteed delivery window of five to seven p.m. that evening.

Her next stop was Target. The super store would have everything she needed to outfit the apartment kitchen and get some linens and other staples for the apartment. Emma loved Target. Before her financial settlement with the New York law firm, it had been her go-to shopping spot. Now, even when money was absolutely no object, she fell back into that old pattern.

She went to the kitchen section first and found some plates, utensils, a modest set of cookware, and a bunch of kitchen gadgets. She went with a blue-and-white color scheme because she liked the abstract pattern of the plates, so she built the rest of the kitchen around that one color.

She used the same color palette for the bathroom, buying towels and bric-a-brac so the white bath wouldn't seem so stark. Her final stop, even though she barely had any room left in her cart, was bedding. This would be a tad trickier. She had no idea what colors the Segans might like for their rooms, but she decided to go with her gut. David's room would be aqua and Jeanine's room would be coral.

Finding the correct comforter and spread for David's room was quick. Emma's overflowing cart was now so full she had to peer around the side of the merchandise in order to navigate the aisles.

She spotted a perfect spread up on a top shelf, but it was far too high for her to reach. She glanced around and noticed a tall ebony-haired girl at the end of the aisle. "Excuse me?" she asked.

Nothing.

"Excuse me?" Emma said, louder.

This time the pretty girl turned around and flashed a beautiful smile. Emma guessed she was about seventeen-ish, so she asked, "Can you tell me what you think of this for a boy's room?" She patted the comforter on top of her precarious pile.

"It's great," she said, and her smile reached her clear blue eyes. "I'm more of a lavender person but I can see a guy liking on that spread."

"Good," Emma breathed. "Could you do me a favor?"

"Sure," the girl said easily.

"Can you get me down that coral bedspread on the top shelf? I don't want to hang around waiting for a salesperson just because I'm too short to reach the frigging thing."

The much taller girl put her cellphone in her back pocket and easily retrieved the bedspread. "Here you go," she said.

Only it wouldn't *go*. There simply wasn't enough room in her cart. "Crap," Emma muttered.

"Let me try to stuff it underneath," she offered.

With a tug here and a shove there, they managed to get the spread under the cart. "Thank you so much."

"Not a prob," she said.

"Thanks to you," Emma reached into her wallet. "Let me give you a little something for your assistance."

The girl held up her hand. "That isn't necessary."

Emma tilted her head to one side and pursed her lips. "How old are you?"

"Sixteen."

"When I was sixteen I *always* needed extra cash. And I really couldn't have completed my shopping without you. Take this."

"Don't you dare," came a familiar male voice from behind Emma. She spun around and found Conner Kavanaugh glaring at her.

"This girl helped me out. I'm just showing my appreciation." She placed one hand on her hip. "What's it to you?" she challenged.

"She's my daughter."

Wow. He doesn't look old enough to have a teenager was her first thought, and the second—*Holy shit, he was hitting on me and he's married*. "So that means she can't accept a gratuity for a job well done?" Emma shot right back at him.

"It's okay," the girl interrupted softly. "I really don't need a tip."

"See what you did?" Emma glared up at Conner's far too handsome face. "You embarrassed her."

"Sam's supposed to be picking out a new bedspread," Conner said. "Not acting as your gofer."

"I'm sure she can multi-task."

"Miss No Husband, No Children is giving me parenting advice?"

"This is stupid," Emma muttered then she reached out and tucked the twenty-dollar bill in the pocket of his uniform. Big mistake. Big, *big* mistake. In that flash of a second she felt rock solid muscle beneath her fingers. Her mind immediately went to a place that had nothing to do with spreads and cutlery, and a lot to do with a bed.

She attempted to make a brisk, intentional departure, except that her cart practically outweighed her and she had to grunt in order to get the damned thing to move. Of course then she heard his deep chuckle and watched as his daughter attempted—badly—to keep a straight face.

Emma couldn't check out fast enough. She kept looking behind her, afraid she'd see Conner again *and* afraid she wouldn't. Did he have to be so hot? And the daughter—was there a wife? Emma didn't think so. Conner didn't seem like the kind of guy who would cheat. He was too Law and Order for that sort of behavior. No, had to be divorced.

Which had its own problems. As a rule, Emma didn't date men with families. Too much potential for drama, and then there was always the secret she guarded.

Her phone vibrated while the clerk was bagging the last of her purchases. *Speaking of secrets…* Emma looked down at the number, knew it was her sister, and let it go to voicemail. She'd call Amelia later, when she was at home and could give her sister her full attention. Translation: listen to her sister grouse about her being in Purdue.

Though she was running out of steam, she made one final stop. She pulled into the Honda dealership and parked in a visitor's spot. She pulled up Truecar.com on her phone and once she had a number in mind, walked inside.

"I'm Jeremy. How can I help you?"

"I want a Honda Civic. Automatic." She paused and looked around the showroom. "In that color green if you have it." She pointed to a light metallic she thought was pretty.

"A woman who knows her mind," Jeremy said in a smarmy car salesman tone. "Let me check."

He was gone for about ten minutes and came back with an eager look on his face. "As it turns out, we do have that model in that color in stock. Come into my office so we can discuss price."

She followed him into a cubicle. He made a production out of taking a legal pad out of the drawer and writing a number at the top of the page. "Let's talk about your trade-in and some financing options."

"I'm not trading my car in and I'm paying cash." She

reached for the legal pad and wrote her own number on it. "I can go twenty miles down the road and get the same car for that price. Match it or I won't take up any more of your time."

"Let me get my general manager," he said.

It took Emma less than five minutes to make the deal at her price with the manager. "Would it be possible to have the car delivered?" she asked.

"We can do that," the manager said. "Around supper-time?"

"That's fine."

Emma needed a nap after all that shopping. By the time she headed back toward home, it was almost four-thirty.

She was excited about her purchases and looked forward to sharing the bounty. That, she decided, was the best part of having money. She'd spent the vast majority of her young life struggling in a single-parent family, then she'd moved on to being a scholarship student at an ivy league school. Now, spreading around her wealth to others was satisfying.

But the past was the past and she intended to keep it that way. Which probably meant she should stop antagonizing Conner Kavanaugh. She didn't want him looking into her past. If he did, it wouldn't take him too long to discover that Emma McKinley didn't exist.

CHAPTER SEVEN

Emma arrived home to find a large moving van in her driveway. Finally, she'd have a real bed instead of the uncomfortable air mattress.

Three very large men off-loaded her dining table and chairs as she slipped inside the house with an armload of packages. Inside the house, Jeanine removed the plastic wrap as each item was brought into the dining room. "This is as fun as Christmas morning," she told Emma, her smile wide and happy. "Your bed is already in place, and made up with those beautiful green sheets, and I'll have this table polished the second I can wrangle off this plastic."

"Wow, you work fast. Everything is coming together beautifully, thanks to you. Nice work, Jeanine."

Jeanine beamed then went back to peeling the plastic off one of the chairs.

Seeing how relaxed the other woman was, Emma knew she'd done the right thing inviting Jeanine and David to live with her. The fact that the woman was helping to make the stark, empty house into a warm and comfortable home was a bonus.

In the living room, David sat on the sofa, an older model laptop in front of him.

Emma couldn't get over the progress. Every room on the first two floors was now furnished. "David?" she asked as she put down the packages beside the new hall table.

He looked up with none of the insolence she had seen on their first meeting. "Yeah?"

"Can you help me with the rest of the bags in my car?"

He set his laptop aside. "Sure."

In no time, they had the Target haul inside and Emma worked side by side with Jeanine to put all the odds and ends in their rightful places. Emma stopped only long enough to tip the movers, then went back to the accessories.

Then she took a little time to admire her new things. The only glaring missing thing was some sort of window treatments, but for now the blinds would have to do. She was all shopped out.

"You have a beautiful home," Jeanine said, standing beside her as they admired their hard work.

"We're not finished yet," she told the other woman with a smile. And as if on cue, the Furniture Barn truck came up the drive.

It took the delivery men about an hour to set up the two third-floor bedrooms and while they were doing that, Emma insisted that Jeanine and David stay away. Emma wanted a big reveal.

"I made jambalaya," Jeanine told her when she came downstairs.

"Is that what I've been smelling all this time?" Emma asked.

Jeanine nodded. What a difference twenty-four hours had made in the woman. She was more relaxed and the puffiness around her blackened eye had subsided somewhat.

Emma washed the new dishes and silverware, dried it, then set the table for three. "Where did you learn to make that?" she asked.

Jeanine smiled. "My people are from southern Louisiana. For me it's comfort food."

"Anything that doesn't come out of the microwave is comfort food for me," Emma teased.

Taking a step back, Jeanine eyed the table. "David and I can eat upstairs."

"Don't be silly," Emma insisted. "Not after you went to all this trouble."

"If you're s—"

"I am."

Jeanine's shoulders relaxed. "I just need to make cornbread and supper will be served."

The Furniture Barn movers found her to sign off on the delivery. "Sounds delish, but hold off on that for a bit," Emma said. She went upstairs for a few minutes to make the beds, then returned and took the woman's arm and called out for David.

The trio climbed the two flights of stairs and as they reached the top, Emma allowed David and his mother to go ahead of her. "If there's anything you don't like…"

"Oh my," Jeanine exclaimed as she covered her gaping mouth.

"Holy shit," David said.

"Like I said, if you don't like anything, we can exchange it."

"I've never had anything so nice before," Jeanine said. "Neither has David. But it's too much," she insisted.

"I had to furnish this house anyway," Emma reasoned. "Having you here just forced me to do it immediately. Besides, I had a lot of fun shopping." *Except for my encounter with Sheriff Kavanaugh.*

"You're too generous, Emma," Jeanine said.

Emma smiled. "And we're not finished yet."

Jeanine eyed her cautiously. "What do you mean?"

She waved her hand. "You'll have to wait."

"Mom!" David called. "Check this out!"

The two women went the short distance to David's room. He was running his hand along the state-of-the-art computer station. "There's a spot here where you put your phone and it charges it."

Emma pointed up to the top shelf of the station. "Did you see your reading material?"

David's smile slipped when he glanced up at the GED prep book. "Not my thing," he said.

"It is now," Emma insisted. "You're too smart to sit around smoking weed and playing video games. Do you want to end up like Skeeter?"

"I'm nothing like him," David countered.

"So prove it," Emma challenged.

David took down the book and skimmed the pages. "I don't understand half of this stuff."

"Then I'll get you a tutor." Emma rubbed her belly. "I'm starving."

"Of course," Jeanine said, scurrying down the stairs.

Emma took advantage of that brief moment alone with David. "You will get your GED."

He tilted his head and gave her a defiant look. "Told you, not my thing."

"Well, I'm telling you it *is* your thing. If you don't put forth the effort, then there's no reason for me to keep employing your mother."

"That's blackmail," he whined.

"That's right." She turned toward the steps. "I have faith in you, David. You'll do the right thing."

"You're a controlling bitch," he muttered with resignation.

"You're not the first person to notice that." Emma followed the wonderful smell to the kitchen and found Jeanine putting a cast iron pan of cornbread in the oven. It smelled divine. While David went back to his computer, Emma decided to use the alone time for her own purposes.

"Did Mrs. Burke like your cooking?" she prodded.

Jeanine stirred the pot. "Not very often. She has a cook. Macy. Been with the family since Mrs. Burke got married."

"So you just cleaned?" Emma asked.

Janine nodded. "Mostly dusting things that didn't need

it. Spent most of my time cleaning the bedrooms."

"Bedrooms?"

"Miss Renae and Mr. Maddison don't share a room. Heck, they don't share much of a life together if you ask me." Jeanine suddenly went red. "I'm sorry, but I don't feel real comfortable speaking out of turn."

Emma raised her hands. "I'm sorry for asking. I was just curious after last night."

"You mean the town council meeting?"

"How did you know about that?"

"I saw Becky at the market today."

"And Becky is?"

"She works at Stella's and Stella told her and then she told me."

"Purdue at its finest," Emma muttered.

"Not much gets left unsaid here," Jeanine agreed. "There's no such thing as a secret in Purdue."

* * *

"Better?" Conner asked when Sam came out of her room.

"Yeah, but can I paint the walls?"

"What color?" he asked as she joined him on the sofa.

"Eggshell."

"That's a color and not a thing?" he asked.

She smiled. "Off white. Clean and minimalist. That's my groove these days."

"But didn't you buy a red bedspread?"

"That's the pop of color," she explained.

Conner nodded. "I'll get the paint and we can do it next weekend."

She pursed her lips for a moment. "C'mon, Dad. It will give me something to do when you're at work."

"I thought you could come to the station with me."

"Ewww! And hang out with the criminals?"

Conner tilted his head back and locked eyes with his daughter. "You used to like coming to my office."

"When I was like five."

"You're going to be here for eight weeks, Sam. You're going to have to come to my office some days."

She tucked a leg under her. "I've been meaning to talk to you about that."

Conner froze, preparing himself in case she was about to ask to leave early. "So talk."

"I want to get a job."

"Doing what?"

She shrugged. "Wait tables, cashiering, shelving books at the library…anything, really. I just want to keep busy and I'd like to earn some money."

"You don't need money. I can support you."

She gave him a playful punch in the arm. "I know that. I'm talking about having my own money, not some handout from you or Barry."

"And how do you propose to get to said job?"

She drew her lower lip between her teeth. "Your old truck?" she suggested.

"That thing is about as reliable as a broken watch."

"But we could fix it up, right?"

Conner breathed in a deep breath and exhaled slowly. "Can I think about it?"

"Yep. Give me your answer by the time I finish de-pinking my room. Speaking of which, can we go to Jake's Hardware before it closes to get the paint?"

"Deal."

It's going to be a very long eight weeks.

* * *

The new car arrived after dinner and Jeanine was reduced to tears when Emma placed the keys in her hand. "It only makes sense," Emma insisted. "You'll be doing most of the errands and the shopping and forgive me, but your car looks like a death trap and I don't know about your motorcycle, but—"

"It's my motorcycle," David injected.

"Does it run?"

He shrugged. "She's a little rough but it gets me from point A to point B."

"It's dangerous," Emma said. "The thing looks like it's put together with spit and chewing gum."

He just shrugged again and Emma made a mental note to consider having it properly repaired. She was about to make that suggestion when her cell rang. It was Amelia. "I have to take this," she said as she excused herself to her office and closed the door. "Hi."

"I've been calling all day," her sister admonished.

"I've been busy," Emma returned. "Has Mom's condition changed?"

"No. But this isn't what she wanted, Emma. You know that."

"I just need to do this first," she argued for the umpteenth time.

"And what *exactly* are you doing?" her sister asked in a huff.

"Research."

"You do that in a library, Em. You don't pick up and move and you sure as hell don't move to Purdue. What if they figure out who you are?"

"What do you think will happen? That the neighbors will come with pitchforks?"

"Go ahead, make jokes, but I'm serious. I'm worried about you."

"There's nothing to worry about," Emma insisted. "All you have to do is keep me updated on Mom's condition while I'm down here."

"I think you're playing with fire. What if this goes public? Did you ever think about what that could do to both of us? It would mean starting over a second time and I don't want to do that. I have friends and a fiancé."

"You really should tell Brody the truth," Emma advised.

"And risk him walking away from me? No way. He asked Amelia McKinley to marry him. Not the daughter of the infamous Courtland Hodges. Look what happened to you in New York when your coworker found out who you really are."

"Yeah, I got rich off a wrongful termination lawsuit."

"And lost everything you'd worked so hard for. Or did

you bust your butt at Harvard to practice law in a backwater town?"

"It's actually very pretty here," she insisted. Her mind instantly produced a picture of Sheriff Kavanaugh. She dismissed it. "I know what I'm doing Amelia. Don't worry."

"I—"

Whatever her sister was about to say was lost in the crackle and boom of a high-powered rifle shot that splintered the window casing and exploded into the room just inches from where she sat.

CHAPTER EIGHT

Instinctively, Emma dropped to the ground and rolled beneath her desk. Shaking, she clutched her phone and huddled in a fetal position waiting for a second shot. *What the hell?* The hard *thud-thud-thud* of her frantic heartbeat echoed loudly in her ears as she braced for another shot.

"Emma?" Jeanine called.

"Stay down!" she yelled.

"I called the police!" Jeanine yelled back.

Emma spent the next several tense minutes breathing deeply and processing what had just happened. She hastily hung up on her sister. *Maybe Amelia's right. Maybe coming to Purdue was a mistake.*

It wasn't until she heard sirens in the distance that she came out of hiding. She was still shaking and her pulse was racing. Moving into the hallway, she found Jeanine and David with stunned looks on their faces.

"Did someone just shoot at us?" David asked.

Emma donned her best smile, trying to reassure the seventeeen-year-old. "I think they were shooting at me," she admitted. The last of her sentence was nearly drowned out by the arrival of the sirens.

With more bravado than she felt, Emma flipped on the porch light then opened the front door. Conner was in the lead, his handsome face deeply lined with concern. Even in her frazzled state, she made mental notes about the man. Hard not to when he was dressed in jeans and T-shirt that hugged his muscular, well-defined torso. Big, broad, armed and dangerous-looking Conner Kavanaugh filled her doorway. She'd never been so happy to see anyone in her life.

He had his hand on the gun at his hip and practically barreled past her into the house. It was then that Emma noticed the young girl in the passenger seat of his SUV.

"You brought your daughter to a crime scene?" she asked incredulously.

"I was the closest unit," he explained. "Show me where the shot came from."

"Right after you bring your daughter inside. What if the crazy person takes another shot? She's out there alone."

Conner sighed heavily, then went and retrieved his daughter. "Emma, this is my daughter, Samantha. Sam."

"Hi," Sam said with a shy smile. She looked a lot like her father. "You're really calm for someone who got shot at."

"Only on the outside," Emma told her. "Follow me." She stopped only long enough to introduce Jeanine and David. "Sam, would you stay with Jeannine and David while I show your dad the window that was shot out?"

Sam hung back with the Segans while Emma escorted the sheriff into the study. He immediately went to the splintered window casing, then walked across the room and squatted down to examine something.

"What is it?" Emma asked.

"Hard to tell. Maybe a .308, maybe an AK. I'll send it to ballistics for testing," he said, taking a latex glove out of his pocket and lifting the misshaped bullet for her to see. It was one hell of a bullet too. Maybe two inches long with a pan-caked end and very lethal looking.

Pressing her hand to her pounding heart, Emma asked, "Is that bullet unusual?" *Dear God, if that bullet had found its target…* A full-body shudder made her grab onto the edge of the desk for support as reality hit. The realization that Connor could've been here investigating her murder chilled her.

"It isn't common. Best I can say is it's from a rifle." He turned and looked at her with those intense gray eyes. "Made any enemies since you arrived?"

She shook her head. "I've only been here a few days. I haven't even had the chance to make a friend, let alone an enemy."

"With the right rifle, this kind of ammo can travel several hundred yards. Could be nothing more than someone firing in the woods and the bullet accidentally striking your house."

Emma felt the tension in her shoulders dissipate. "And here I thought buying this house in the middle of the woods was going to be quiet."

He smiled. It was enough to turn her legs to jelly. Her heart rate quickened and her breath seemed to be caught in her throat. But the worst part was her brain. All notes to self aside, she couldn't look at him without thinking carnal thoughts. She'd never experienced this sort of reaction to a man. But did it have to be this man? At this time? Seriously?

Conner rose to his full six feet four inches and said, "It's virtually impossible for me to say for sure, but I think this is probably nothing more than some jerk out shooting without knowing the range of the weapon."

"Are you sure?"

"I can't be positive, but if you don't have any enemies…"

"I don't." *At least not unless someone knows who I really am.*

He held up the bullet. "I'll go put this into an evidence bag."

Conner turned and in profile, Emma could see his expression change and go rigid. She looked beyond him and saw Sam and David with their heads together.

"Sam, go to the car."

His daughter looked up and gave him an insolent look. Her eyes were intensely blue just as Conner's were intensely gray.

"Stay for coffee," Emma said impulsively. "After all, if you came out here for nothing, I can at least make it worth your while."

"I'd kill for some coffee," Sam said.

"Me too," David added.

Conner gave the young man a withering glare but David didn't seem to care.

"I'll start the pot," Jeanine said, then disappeared into the kitchen.

Conner moved into the hallway, probably hoping his sheer size would intimidate David. It didn't work. Emma found the whole unspoken interchange between father and daughter amusing. Sam clearly had her father's stubborn streak.

In no time Jeanine had served up coffee in the living room. Emma and the Segans sat on one sofa while Sam and Conner sat opposite them. Sam had her head down and was texting away. Every few seconds Emma noticed the young girl would sneak a quick glance at David. There was a crackle of tension in the air but it had very little to do with the teenagers in the room. Conner was silently watching Emma's every move. His eyes locked on her mouth as she took each sip of coffee. It was unnerving and exhilarating all at once. Without moving anything but his gaze, Emma felt as if he was caressing her with his eyes. It was more sensual than a kiss. But being this turned on by merely a hot look was not a good idea.

To break the deafening silence, Emma asked, "Sam, tell me about yourself."

She shrugged. "Not much to tell. I'm in high school and I live most of the year with my mom and stepfather in Chicago."

"She's being modest," Conner added. "She's in a magnet math and science academy. By the time she graduates she'll also have earned two years of college credits."

"Impressive." Emma had an idea. "Have you ever tutored?"

Sam said, "I'm a peer tutor at my school. Advanced math, mostly."

"David needs a tutor."

David turned a little pink. "I have to get my GED."

Sam smiled and became animated. "I can totally help you with that."

"No. You can't," Conner interjected.

"Dad," she whined. "I have a lot of time on my hands while you're at work. This will give me something constructive to do."

"This kid has a record. I'm not leaving you alone with him."

"They won't be alone. Jeanine will be here," Emma promised. "It's a win-win."

"Out of the question," Conner stated flatly. "Like I said, he has a history with the police."

Emma rolled her eyes. "A history that includes flushing a bag of oregano down the toilet right under your nose. You can't fault him for your shortcomings."

"Besides," Sam chimed in. "Don't you want people to treat Uncle Michael well when he gets paroled?"

"Uncle Michael?" Emma queried.

"None of your business," Conner said curtly. He breathed in, then let it out slowly. "You can do the tutoring."

Sam placed her mug on the table and hugged her father around the neck. "Thank you, Daddy."

"But Jeanine or Miss McKinley have to be here. Deal?"

"Totally."

"David?" Conner asked, gaining the teen's attention. "Watch yourself."

"Whatever," he replied.

Jeanine elbowed him in the ribs.

"I mean, yeah," David amended.

"Can we start next week?" Emma asked.

Sam smiled. "That's perfect! I have to paint my bedroom, but other than that I'm totally open."

"Sweet," David said.

"Disaster," Conner grumbled.

"More coffee?" Jeanine asked.

Conner stood and Sam followed his lead. "No," he said. "We need to get going."

"Sorry you came out here for no reason," Emma commented as she also stood.

He shrugged, which pulled the cloth of his shirt taut against his muscled body. Emma swallowed. Hard. But she couldn't rid her mind of wandering into inappropriate territory.

"It wasn't for no reason. Want me to recommend someone to fix that window casing?"

Emma shook her head. "I have a handyman starting tomorrow."

"Willis Maddox?" he asked.

"How did you know that?"

He grinned. "We were just at Jake's Hardware Store and the clerk sold some supplies to Willis, who told him. Then the clerk told Jake, then he told me."

The downfall of small towns. Emma huffed out a puff of air. "Your town has too much time on its hands."

He shrugged again. "What can I say? The community is always curious about newcomers."

On that note he and Sam left the house. The trio set down to a simple dinner, then Jeanine cleaned up the kitchen, and she and David retired to their respective rooms. Emma went back into the study and retrieved her briefcase. She reached inside and pulled out a manila envelope. Taking out the news clippings she reread them for the umpteenth time.

There were articles from the *Washington Post* and the *New York Times*, as well as several from the *Purdue Herald Weekly*.

Some were from twenty years ago, when Emma and her twin sister had been eleven. She could close her eyes and remember that day as if it had happened only hours earlier. Her very normal, peaceful young life had been destroyed that day.

The *Post* article was the most detailed. It explained how the President of the United States had come to Purdue to campaign for the governor. Then, according to the papers, a crazed lone gunman had opened fire on the dais, killing the president and wounding the governor. Kenny Simms, a Purdue deputy, had fired on the gunman, killing him with a single shot to the head. A rifle recovered at the scene had been determined the murder weapon. Case closed, and the country mourned for their popular, fallen leader.

Some of the later articles were from the *Purdue Herald*. Those addressed everything from the initial incident to coverage over the years. There were even anniversary editions, usually featuring Governor Rossner's memories of the day. Those had stopped a few years back when Rossner passed away. In more recent editions, the *Herald* relied heavily on the recollections of Maddison Burke for their retrospective stories. Burke had been the governor's campaign manager.

Emma had received the first clipping in the mail nearly six months ago. There was no return address on the envelope, just a Purdue postmark. Obviously, someone in Purdue knew who she was, but who her sender was was still a mystery. To date, no one had stepped forward or made contact in person.

She assumed someone had gotten wind of the news of the wrongful termination case and then somehow learned about her new identity. That was the only thing that made sense. Her mother had gone to extraordinary lengths to change their identities after the assassination. They had even moved from Washington, D.C. to a small town in north Georgia. Emma and Amelia had made it through high school and college without anyone learning their secret.

Emma ran her fingertips over the single word written atop each clipping. *Why?*

She sighed as she looked at the assassin's photo. "'Why' is right. Daddy, why did you do it?"

CHAPTER NINE

Conner slept fitfully and awakened well before dawn. Visiting days were always stressful, but his bimonthly visit to Jarretsville wasn't what had him on edge. No, he definitely had Emma McKinley on the brain.

As his coffeepot slowly dripped into the carafe, he closed his eyes and conjured her image. She was beautiful, he acknowledged. Blond hair, blue eyes, and legs that inspired fantasies. But the other night she'd been different, at least for a little while, when he'd first arrived. She had a soft vulnerability about her that he found very appealing and really intriguing. He could think of a lot of adjectives to describe her, but "vulnerable" hadn't been among them. No, she was also confident, even cocky. And that carried its own appeal.

During her first week in Purdue, she'd not lost a motion or a case. He'd snuck over a time or three to the court to watch her in action. She was laser focused and knew the law better than anyone in the room. So why, he wondered again, had she opted to come to Purdue? He loved his hometown and its slow pace, but she didn't have any connection to the north Florida town.

Elgin Hale said she'd come from New York City and Conner had a hard time reconciling why a woman would leave the fast pace of New York for a small town. Without divulging a number, Frances at the bank had shared with Yolanda, who'd shared with his secretary, that Emma was their biggest client. Which only added fuel to his intrigue. Why would a rich woman choose Purdue? Was she hiding? From what or whom? Avoiding an overzealous lover? He didn't like the thought of her having a lover, and the fact that he felt that way about a relative stranger—no matter how sexy and appealing—freaked him out a little.

Last night's shooting bothered him. He'd made light of it to Emma, but maybe that had been a mistake. Even if some fool had accidentally fired that shot—what the hell was he doing in the woods at that time of night?

He pondered those thoughts and sipped strong coffee for the better part of two hours until Sami—er, Sam—appeared in the kitchen. "Morning Dad." She kissed the top of his head. "Coffee?"

"In the pot," he said. "Mugs are in the cabinet above the coffee maker."

Sam poured a cup, doctored it with some cream and sugar, then joined him at the round kitchen table that he had inherited from his grandmother. In fact, most of his décor was rustic. Except for the fifty-inch flat screen hanging in the family room.

"What time are we leaving to go see Uncle Michael?" she asked.

"I'd like to be on the road at eight-thirty."

Sam gulped down her coffee. "I'm going to shower."

She was almost down the hallway when he called, "I've got a gathering to go to tonight. Are you okay with being alone for a little while?"

"Dad! I'm not a toddler. Besides, I'm going to be painting my room."

He wasn't even sure why he'd been invited. It wasn't as if the Burkes made a habit of inviting him to their home. So, he was going more out of curiosity than anything else. Plus he knew Emma would be there.

It took him all of fifteen minutes to shower, shave and dress in jeans and a button-down shirt. Sam, on the other hand, didn't emerge from her room until five minutes before departure time. She looked very grown up a short dress with what she called leggings, and some ballet flats. They reminded him of her time in dance classes which, looking at her now, seemed like a lifetime ago. "Ready?" he asked.

The drive to Jarrettsville took less than an hour. The last twenty miles was pine forest dotted with the occasional trailer home, then rather abruptly a large, heavily fortified wall topped with razor wire soared twenty feet in the air before them.

Once they parked, they passed through a series of security stations. Conner had gone through this procedure enough times to know to leave his gun locked in his SUV. He greeted various correctional officers he had gotten to know over the past fifteen years.

Along with a few dozen other visitors, Conner and Sam were ushered into a common room. It smelled of bleach and stale coffee. There were at least fifty stainless steel tables bolted to the floor. Michael had been a model prisoner so far; he'd earned the right to see them in the visitors' center instead of in the glass booths with handsets like in his early years here.

Conner felt his heart clench as he waited for his older brother. Sam must have sensed something because she reached over and squeezed his hand.

"There he is," she said a minute later when Michael came into the room.

Conner shook his hand; it was the only permitted physical contact allowed by the prison. "Hey," he said as they shook hands. Conner looked him up and down. "You're starting to look like Declan," he joked.

Michael shook his head. "I have a lot of time to work out," he replied. "But not enough to look like him. Last time he was here he looked like he'd just stepped out of Seal Team Six."

"How are they treating you?" Sam asked.

"I'm fine, honey. Especially seeing you. Man, you've grown up since the last time I saw you."

"Tell him that," she joked as she hooked a thumb in her father's direction.

Conner felt his gut clench. "What day is your parole hearing?"

"Two weeks from Monday," Michael answered, though his voice was tinged with a hint of resignation. "The chances that they'll let me out on my first time up for parole are slim."

"Well, Declan and Jack are coming up and Sam and I will be there, so you can show them you have a complete support system on the outside."

"Thanks, brother."

They spent two hours catching up. Sam talked about her school, while Conner filled him in on Jack's recent engagement to Darby Hayes. They talked until the siren went off, indicating that visiting hours were over.

When they left, Conner felt the usual sense of helplessness. Michael had spent fifteen years inside that prison for a crime that wasn't his fault. Conner still vividly remembered that night years ago, when his father had been abusing his mother—his favorite pastime—and Michael stepped in. They'd struggled for the gun and it discharged, hitting their mother in the chest. She died instantly. Michael was still wrestling for the weapon when it discharged for a second time, killing their father. Even though he'd been only seventeen, he'd been charged as an adult. Michael had been convicted on two counts of voluntary manslaughter and given a twenty-five-year sentence.

Jack and Conner had been sent to live with an aunt and uncle in Purdue. They'd been good people and they'd provided a nice home for the boys. Conner still missed them.

"Are you going to be quiet all the way home?" Sam asked.

"Sorry, baby," he said, reaching over to pat her knee. "I just get bummed out seeing him like that."

"But he'll get paroled, right?"

Conner nodded. "Eventually."

"Well, that sucks."

* * *

Emma was trying to decide what to wear. She had three dresses laid out on her bed. One was a simple but classic little black dress. One was a red cocktail dress with sexy but discrete cutouts. The third was a white dress with a plunging back. "I like all of you," she told the clothes. "Note to self: don't talk to your outfits."

Each had its plusses, which was why making this decision was so difficult. She needed a second opinion so she called Jeanine into her room.

"Which one?" she asked as one by one she held each dress against herself.

"The white one, definitely."

Emma turned it around and showed her the back. "Are you sure I won't be showing too much skin?"

Jeanine shook her head. "It's pretty and with your figure, it will be very flattering."

"But aren't the Burkes kind of…conservative?" she asked.

"Trust me, Maddison Burke will *love* that dress and Renae will be pea green with envy. She's almost sixty now, so she can't get away with such a revealing dress." Jeanine smiled. "I'd like to be a fly on the wall when she gets a look at you."

"Was she that difficult to work for?"

"You have no idea," Jeanine answered on a rush of breath.

"What about Maddison? How is he?"

Jeanine shook her head. "Pathetic. She calls all the shots and he takes all the glory. Can you imagine what he'll be like as a senator? If you ask me, he's too weak and too dependent on his wife to be in Congress. But I also think that's just a stepping stone. I think Renae has her eyes on the White House. He's going to win that senate seat," she said with resignation. "They put on a perfect face for the public. You'll see tonight."

It took Emma only thirty minutes to do her hair and makeup, then slip on the dress. She chose a pair of nude heels, left the house, and entered the Burkes' address into her car's navigation system. The drive would take her seventeen minutes, which should get her there close to the time on the invitation she'd received in the mail.

Following the instructions on the invitation, she reached an ornate gate and a callbox, illuminated by her headlights. Reaching out of the window, she pressed the button and announced herself. The gates swung open like the jaws of an alligator.

Taking a couple of deep breaths as she drove up the long drive, Emma realized she was starting to get nervous. Spanish moss dripped off the branches of huge live oaks that guarded either side of the roadway like soldiers, and as she neared the house she slowed in order to take it all in.

The house was a giant Victorian with a huge and perfectly manicured front lawn. The wraparound porch held window boxes that spilled purple petunias over the white railings. The din of conversation and the gentle sounds of a piano playing drifted out on the balmy evening air. The fragrance of roses, the ghosts of multiple perfumes, and the enticing aroma of food welcomed her.

A valet greeted her as she stepped out of her car. "Thank you." She handed him her keys then climbed the seven steps up to enter the open front doorway.

"Opulent" didn't begin to describe the place. It wasn't to her taste, but Emma had to admit that Renae Burke had carefully decorated the home with pieces true to its period—which translated into a lot of gilding. She was in the foyer and just to her left was a majestic staircase winding up to the second floor. To her right was a long hallway and a parlor. A uniformed woman greeted her and handed her a glass of champagne with a raspberry in the glass.

Emma took a sip. It was wonderful champagne, and based on the other good aromas she expected she was in for a culinary treat as well.

"This way, please."

Emma followed the server through the house and out a back entrance. The backyard was as lovely as the front, but it was crowded with many of the people she had met at Stella's on her first day in Purdue. She was descending the steps, admiring the twinkle lights as she did, when she felt all eyes turn in her direction. She hated being the center of attention, and it suddenly occurred to her that she should probably have worn the black dress. *Damn.* Tilting her chin, she kept going.

The din grew softer and the piano music louder. Renae Burke separated herself from one modest group and started in her direction. The older woman wore a beautiful silk dress in a deep jade that highlighted her green eyes.

Smiling, she gave Emma air kisses on either cheek. It was creepy.

"Thank you for coming," Renae said.

"I wouldn't have missed it."

"Me either," came a deep voice from behind her.

She glanced back to see Conner on the top step. He was wearing a suit, which was both good and bad. Good in the sense that his appearance showed her a different side of him, but bad because he looked positively sexy in a dark suit and a crisp white shirt. It showed off his dark coloring and some-how made his gray eyes seem more intense. Predictably, her body responded even though her brain tried push away the thoughts.

He came down to where she stood, a glass of champagne in one hand, and offered the other to Renae. "Thank you for the invitation."

"Why, Sheriff, you are always welcome here."

Once they had shaken hands, one of the staff members interrupted and requested Renae's presence in the kitchen. When she went off to tend to whatever emergency had cropped up, Conner asked, "Shall we mingle?"

"I suppose. This really isn't my thing."

"Mine either," he said.

Conner placed his hand at her back. Skin to skin. His splayed fingers against her naked skin sent her pulse up a notch. Even the cool evening air couldn't stop the heat from coursing through her veins. She felt his touch with every coiled nerve in her body.

She tried to step away but he stuck to her. "Do you have to do that?" she asked in an amazingly steady voice.

"Do what?"

"Touch me."

"You're the one who came half-dressed." His fingers began to make sensual little motions on her back. "Which isn't a criticism. I'm enjoying myself."

She reached around and removed his hand. "I'm not here for your enjoyment."

"Sure you are. You're the whole reason for this little gathering."

"I was already introduced to most of these people."

"Introduced, yes. Observed, no."

"Observe me doing what?"

"Anything. Everything. Renae is probably freaked because you have more money than she does. She's used to being queen bee."

"And does anyone know how much money I have?"

"I don't know the exact amount. Just that you're the bank's best customer. A title Renae has held for decades."

"Let me guess." She looked up in order to meet his gaze. "You know somebody who knows somebody who knows somebody at the bank."

He smiled.

Her legs threatened to turn to jelly. "You have an incestuous town, Sheriff."

"Conner," he corrected. "And I should be mad at you."

"For what?"

"Having my daughter tutor your charity case David Segan."

She shook her head. "Don't you believe in second chances?"

"Not when you have a rap sheet that predates puberty."

"Nickle-and-dime dumb stuff. But that's the thing. David is a smart kid whose only real crime was being raised in a shit home environment."

"And Maddox? You hired him because…"

"Practical self-interest," she explained. "I don't have any man skills. Maddox takes care of almost everything."

"Almost?"

She shrugged. "He can't fix the window casing."

"I can."

She eyed him skeptically. "And why would you want to come to my house and repair my window?"

"I'm neighborly that way."

She thought for a minute. "You just want to be there when Sam tutors David."

He simply shrugged. Well, it wasn't all that simple. The action accentuated his broad shoulders and narrow hips. And it didn't help that his woodsy cologne was wafting in her direction. "Guilty."

"Does your daughter know you don't trust her?"

His expression hardened. "It isn't her I don't trust. It's the Segan kid I have doubts about."

"Then come fix my window. You'll see David in a whole new light."

"Speaking of light," he said in a sexy, lowered voice. "You look beautiful in the moonlight."

"You clean up well, too," she answered quickly before the lump of desire in her throat hindered her ability to speak. "Let's mingle."

He put his hand on her back again and kept it there, making it nearly impossible for her to remember who was who. All she could do was imagine what it would be like to have him peel her dress off and make love to her all night.

Maybe Amelia was right. Obviously, Purdue was full of mine fields, the biggest one being Conner Kavanaugh. She hadn't expected someone like him and she wasn't completely sure how to handle the situation before it derailed her from her goal.

CHAPTER TEN

The Burkes' backyard had been transformed with small LED lights strung from the porch through the trees. Several linen-covered round tables dotted the lawn. A baby grand was out on the far end of the porch and a tuxedo-clad pianist played a steady stream of classical music.

Emma guessed there were about twenty-five guests. She remembered some of them from her quick meet-and-greet at Stella's. Her boss, Elgin Hale, was among them and Emma recognized the petite woman with him as his wife. There was a framed picture of her in Elgin's office. Hayden Blackwell was there as well, and he was headed in her direction.

Emma took a long swallow of her champagne then said, "Good evening Mr. Blackwell."

"Call me Hayden," he insisted as he turned his attention to Conner, who was still standing sentry over her. Annoying man. "Sheriff. Mind if I borrow her for a few minutes?"

"I'm not the sheriff's to lend," Emma said tartly before

following the State's Attorney to an empty table without looking back. One of the uniformed waitstaff came by with a tray of mini quiches. Another replaced her empty flute with a full one. "What do you need?" Emma asked.

"The LeFabre case," he answered.

"What about it?" Emma said as she reviewed the case in her mind. It was about a dog. Her client, Jeff LaFabre, had started a fight outside a strip club. It had erupted into a brawl, with Jeff smack in the middle of it. During the chaos, one man had been stabbed and he later died at the hospital. Jeff had been identified by two of the other combatants as the person with the knife.

"I have a strong case," Blackwell began. "But I'm feeling generous. Your client pleads to one count of voluntary manslaughter with a deadly weapon and I agree to a sentence recommendation of fifteen years."

Emma smiled and chuckled softly. "You have a weak case dependent on the testimony of two guys so drunk they had a hard time telling the cops their names. The night of the fight they both swore they couldn't identify the person with the knife. Then the Crime Stoppers reward gets posted and suddenly they're fonts of information? They have a reason to lie. Either one of them could be the actual killer. Without video surveillance, there's no way you can corroborate their statements. I've got enough reasonable doubt to drive a truck through."

Hayden's eyes narrowed and his neck began to turn red above his too-tight white collar. "What kind of plea are you looking for?"

For all her outward bravado, Emma knew she had one major problem: her client. He was a big, beefy guy covered in tattoos. And they weren't limited to his body. No, Jeff had teardrop facial tattoos and some sort of tribal thing covering one side of his face. Truth be told, any jury would take one look at him and presume he was guilty of something. "I can only recommend this to my client."

"I understand."

"Involuntary manslaughter. No weapons charge. Five years."

Hayden scoffed. "He killed a man."

Emma smiled. "Allegedly. I can line up a dozen witnesses from that night to say it was impossible to tell who did the stabbing because there were at least a dozen guys fighting in that parking lot."

"Ten years," Hayden countered.

Emma shook her head. "Seven."

Hayden sucked in a deep gulp of cool night air. "Okay. Sell it to your client and then send me the paperwork."

"Why, Hayden Blackwell," came a familiar female voice.

Emma turned around and saw Renae walking up to them. She had a stern look in her eyes as she said, "This is a party. Not a time for you two to be working."

"Sorry, Renae," Hayden said. "It was just a small matter I thought we could resolve quickly."

The older woman hooked her arm through Emma's and steered her back toward the group. "There are some more people I want you to meet. I can't tell you how sorry I am that Hayden sidetracked you. This is a party, for heaven's sake."

"It was no big deal," Emma assured her. She could practically taste the other woman's perfume as she looked up and admired the lovely home. "Your home is amazing," she said.

"Thank you, we like it. We had it built when my husband was in his second term as governor and we were living in Tallahassee. I love Victorian; it took over a year to build and furnish. I tried to keep it as authentic as possible. I even went to England to get some of the furniture and artwork."

"I'd love a full tour," Emma said.

Renae was beaming. "Of course. Let me make a few more introductions and then I'll take you inside."

Emma found herself scanning the guests for Conner. He was having a conversation with Wayne the bailiff. He looked good in that suit. She was admiring him openly when he suddenly glanced her way. Emma immediately averted her gaze and gave herself a little mental bitch slap for allowing herself to be distracted by him.

Renae introduced her to a half-dozen people, mostly local businessmen and women. At some point she'd been handed another flute of champagne, along with a wonderful caviar bite that exploded with flavor in her mouth. Rubbing elbows with the wealthy definitely had its perks.

Emma was new to the world of money. Settling the lawsuit had ended her career in New York but it had put more than twenty million dollars in her bank account. For a person who'd been a scholarship student at an elite private boarding school for girls, and later at Harvard, her new-found wealth was like the entry into another universe. Having money gave her freedom. Including the freedom to explore Purdue.

"…is Kenny Simms," Renae was saying.

Emma froze for a minute as she looked at the man standing in front of her. He reminded her of Bruce Willis. He was maybe six feet tall, bald, and in amazing shape for a man in his fifties. He was also the man who had killed her father.

She recovered quickly. "Nice to meet you," she said, shaking his hand.

"Kenny is my husband's chief of security."

Who needed a chief of security in Purdue? What were the Burkes afraid of? "I've never met a security expert," Emma said. "What exactly do you do?" she inquired.

He regarded her with steely dark eyes. "It varies."

Renae reached out and gave Emma's hand a squeeze. "Kenny keeps the crazies at bay. He's been with us since Maddison was in the state house and we lured him away from the police department when Maddison decided to explore a campaign for the senate."

"So your husband is running?"

Renae just smiled non-committally. "Shall we go inside?"

Emma plastered a smile on her face and said to the man, "Nice to have met you." Then she followed Renae up the porch steps.

"The house is ten thousand square feet with seven bedrooms and eight baths," her hostess said as they weaved through the busy, state-of-the-art kitchen.

Emma was shown the perfectly appointed parlor, the living room, and the dining room with its twenty-five-foot table. It was impressive but for her taste there was too much gilding, with a lot of burgundy accents and textured wallpaper all over the place.

Renae gave her little history lessons along the way. She explained the derivation of certain pieces of furniture and recited the accomplishments of the various artists who'd sculpted or painted their way into her home. There was one painting in particular that struck Emma. It was a watercolor of a large series of villas set on the bank of a marsh. Renae identified the artist, so Emma assumed it had been, like the small Renoir in the dining room, copied, or perhaps in one of her art books from school.

The second story was just as impressive. The master bedroom especially looked like a scaled-down version of a chamber out of Versailles. Emma could just close her eyes and imagine Renae lounging on the velvet chaise, eating peeled grapes while relaxing with a magazine. Again the colors were off-putting, but Emma could appreciate the quality, if not the style.

Renae showed her Maddison's study, which had a beautiful view of the backyard with all the magnolia trees. The study's walls were lined with awards and framed photographs. One in particular caught her eye. It was a picture of Renae and Maddison with the President and First Lady. Judging by their clothing, the photo had to have been taken on the same day as the assassination.

"It is truly a beautiful home," she told Renae as they

stood at the top of the grand staircase to admire the chandelier Renae had commissioned from a glassblower in Seattle.

"I understand you bought the Franklin home."

"Yes," Emma said.

Renae sighed. "Not to be rude but I also understand you've hired Jeanine Segan."

"Yes."

"I know you're new in town, but I wish you would've called me before you hired her."

"Why?" Emma asked, playing dumb.

"She used to work for me and unfortunately we discovered she was stealing from us."

"Stealing what?"

"Coins, jewelry, cash."

"I did a background check and nothing came up."

Renae gave a little shrug. "We couldn't make an official complaint. Jeanine was very good at covering her tracks. We didn't have the evidence to prove she was a thief."

"Without evidence—"

"Oh, it had to be her," Renae cut in. "The dates that things went missing coincided with the days Jeanine worked."

"Only Jeanine?" Emma asked.

"Well, technically no. But the only other person with unrestricted access to the house was my cook, Mary, and she's been with us since we were first married. I trust her implicitly."

"I'm comfortable with my decision," Emma replied, then took a small sip of champagne.

"I also understand you've hired that pitiful homeless man."

"Willis Maddox?"

"You are far more trusting than I am," Renae said. "Then again, safety is of paramount concern for us."

"That's alarming," Emma said with just the right amount of concern. "What happened to make you extra cautious?"

"We had an incident years ago that left us shaken. Suffice to say we take security very seriously."

Emma wanted to hear Renae's version of the events. "May I ask—"

Emma knew from the news clippings that Renae and Maddison had had front row seats for the *incident*. Maddison had been the then-governor's campaign manager and he'd been next to the dais when the shots rang out. He had gone on to lead his own political career; moving from state senate up to governor. Now he had his sights set on the U.S. Senate.

"We never talk about it." Renae waved her hand, the diamonds in her rings flashing in the light. "Shall we rejoin the party?"

As soon as Emma was back outside, she discovered Conner seemed to be waiting for her. He was at her side in a matter of seconds. And he wasn't the only one following her every move. In her absence, Bill Whitley had arrived and was standing with their boss. Her coworker was staring at her with nearly open hostility. It was perfectly clear that he didn't like having her around.

The other set of eyes latched on to her belonged to Kenny Simms. His face was completely expressionless, so she didn't know what his issue might be. Surely he didn't see her as a threat to the Burkes' security.

"How did you like it?" Connor asked.

She shrugged. "It's nice. A little too ornate for my taste. What's the story on the Simms guy?"

"He used to be with the Purdue Police Department. Then he switched to the Florida State Troopers and eventually ended up on Governor Burke's security detail when Maddison was in the state house."

"Renae told me that. I'm just curious about why they *need* security."

"Paranoia," Conner supplied.

"That is just silly. Purdue seems like a pretty quiet town." She silently hoped he might mention the assassination. No such luck.

"Someone shot at your house a few days ago," he reminded her.

A chill danced along her exposed spine. "I thought you said it was some sportsman's errant shot." And if she told herself it was a random shooting enough times, maybe one day she'd believe it. But Emma was waiting for another shoe to drop.

"I'm sure it was. By the way, you should have Willis put up some new *No Trespassing* and *No Hunting* signs around your property. That house was vacant for a long time and people got used to using those woods to hunt and shoot."

"My realtor failed to mention that," Emma commented.

"Just post the signs. You shouldn't have any other problems."

The party wound down and that was just fine with Emma. It wasn't until she was in her car and on the way home that she felt her muscles begin to uncoil. She reached her driveway and carefully drove up to the darkened house. She was guided only by the lamplight from the third story.

As she reached the front door with her key out, her breath caught in her throat and she stopped short. A single white tulip with its stem dipped in blood was lying on the porch in front of the closed door.

CHAPTER ELEVEN

Emma's first thought upon seeing the blood-dipped flower was to call Connor. Not just because he was the sheriff, but because having a big, muscled guy with a loaded weapon with her right now would help dispel her nerves. But she rejected that.

First, because she was used to fighting her own damned battles, second because she'd just seen him, and third, she did not want him thinking she was a freaking damsel in distress.

There wasn't anything he could do, but there was something she could do for herself.

She unlocked the door and discovered the house was quiet. She assumed Jeanine and David were in their respective rooms. Before stepping over the threshold, she plucked the flower off the porch and immediately deposited it in the garbage as she passed through the kitchen.

"Note to self: install video cameras." The sound of her

own voice in the quiet house was comforting as she washed her hands.

She was still keyed up after the party, partly because she was intrigued by the variety of people she'd met and partly because she could still feel the ghost of Conner Kavanaugh's fingers dancing along her bare back. Emma shivered. Not an *I'm cold* shiver. Nope, this was primal lust. A distraction and a complication she couldn't afford.

Maybe the flower person was the same person who'd sent her the clippings. It was a possibility, but a grim one. Emma had thought that once she arrived in Purdue, the anonymous clippings sender might contact her in some fashion. If the blood-dipped flowers constituted contact, she was stumped.

She slipped off her heels and went into her office. She retrieved the news clippings and scanned them again, trying to see if there was any mention of flowers. Nothing. Just like there was no explanation as to how her father had ended up at the presidential rally that night. All she knew was that he had responded to a timeshare invitation in Purdue and had somehow ended up murdering the leader of the free world. She returned the clippings to her briefcase.

Emma opened her laptop and waited the ridiculously long time it took for the relatively new machine to come to life. While it did its thing, she decided to make herself a cup of coffee. She was startled when she turned the corner into the kitchen from the hall and found David in the kitchen.

"You scared me," she said.

"Sorry."

"No big deal. I'll just tie a bell around your neck so I'll know when you're around."

He gave her a small grin. "Why do I think you'd actually do something so whack?" he asked. "And I know I'm supposed to stay upstairs, but my mom hasn't stocked our fridge yet and I'm hungry."

"David, you can have the run of the place. Except for my office and my bedroom."

He shrugged. "How was the party?"

"Long."

"I'll bet. When my mother worked for the Burkes she put in some long hours and usually got screwed on her paycheck."

"I can see Renae stiffing an employee. She seems like a bit of a tight ass."

He raised a speaking brow. "Only a bit?"

It was Emma's turn to shrug. "Did you happen to notice anyone outside the house tonight? Maybe hear a noise or something?"

He shook his head. "No, but I had on headphones with the music jacked, so I didn't hear anything other than my tunes." He took the container of leftover jambalaya from the fridge, nudging the door closed with his hip. "Why?"

Emma sighed. "Nothing major. Someone in the area is screwing with me."

"Welcome to Purdue," David said with a snort of disgust. "Now you understand why I bailed on school. This town is toxic."

"So, get your GED and go to some college far away from Purdue."

He gave her a sidelong glance. "And pay for it how?"

"Student loans, scholarships…I'd be happy to help you once you get your GED."

He squinted and he looked at her with mistrust. "What's your deal? First you give my mom and me someplace to live. Then you throw in a car. And now you're offering me help with college?"

Emma smiled. "Trust me, this has nothing to do with you. I grew up with a single mom who worked two jobs just to keep us in a decent apartment."

"You didn't grow up rich?"

"Nope. I've been where you are and I know what it takes to break the cycle. You're smart, David. Get an education and decide what you want to do and you're all set."

"I already know what I want to do."

"You do?" Emma asked, a tad surprised, looking up from popping a pod into the coffee machine. Then she leaned against the counter, waiting for the Keurig to do its magic.

"I want to work in the tech industry." He paused as if expecting her to mock him. "I'm self-taught but I'm pretty good with computers. I've already taught myself basic code."

"That's great," Emma said. "Does that mean you can fix my slow computer? It's taking forever to load."

He nodded. "Sure. Is it in your office?"

While they were chatting, Emma's the coffeepot spewed into her mug and she soon had a steaming mug of coffee in her hands. "Follow me," she said.

Emma stood off to the side, giving David the chair. His fingers flew across the keyboard and the screen turned blue. Then a bunch of numbers and symbols scrolled across the screen, making Emma nervous. "Are you sure you know what you're doing?"

"Piece of cake," he assured her. "You've got too many programs loading when you turn the machine on. If we delete some of them, your computer will operate much faster."

To Emma's ears what he said sounded like *Wah wah wah*. The information went right over her head. When it came to computers, she knew how to use the power button and that was about it.

"You have two versions of security software. Which one do you want to keep?"

He might as well have asked her to explain advanced math theory. "Whichever one works better."

"Actually, I have a better one. Hang on and I'll go get my thumb drive."

She could hear David's heavy footfalls as he ascended and descended two flights of stairs. He returned to her office and in just a few minutes had a new security system loaded on her computer.

"Try it now," he said, surrendering the chair.

Thanks to David, the laptop came to life in roughly one-quarter of the time. "You're amazing," she said.

David blushed slightly. "It was nothing."

"Not to me," she assured him. "Go feed yourself. You've earned it."

Once David was gone, Emma set about doing some

Google searches. Maddison Burke had an elaborate website set up for his campaign. Emma read about his various positions as well as his long biography. The site was also littered with photographs taken of Burke through the years. Renae was in most of them—usually standing politely next to him, always impeccably dressed. Emma noticed something else as well. Or rather *someone* else. Former deputy Kenny Simms was in several of the pictures. Since he was the one who had killed her father following the assassination, Emma had to admit she was curious about him. Why had he used a kill shot? Where did her father get the rifle? Her rational mind reminded her that her father was the assassin and Simms had only been doing his duty. Still, it was difficult to look at pictures of the man.

Not wanting to dwell on the past, she searched lilies and tulips to try to understand why someone would be taunting her with those specific bloody flowers. She didn't find anything aside from planting tips and places to order bulbs; eventually she gave up and went to bed.

* * *

She got up early, knowing Conner and his daughter were coming over: Conner to fix her window casing and Sam to begin tutoring David. Though she refused breakfast, Jeanine insisted she have a freshly made sweet roll along with her three cups of coffee. Emma reminded Jeanine she had the day off but Jeanine insisted she didn't need it.

After putting on jeans and a pale blue, long-sleeved

T-shirt, she spent a few extra minutes on her makeup as anticipation knotted her stomach. For a smart woman, she knew she was being very stupid. Her stay in Purdue was temporary at best, and as soon as the sheriff found out who she was he'd probably run for the woods.

After twisting her hair up in a messy bun, she went down to the kitchen and pulled the telephone book from the drawer. Looking up alarm services, she chose one with Sunday and evening hours and gave them a call. She'd just placed the receiver back on the cradle when the doorbell chimed.

Her stomach fluttered and she stood planted in place, listening to Jeanine's soft footfalls and the *snick* of the latch as she opened the front door. Emma put on a fresh cup of coffee.

Conner filled the doorway. She had intended to only give him a quick glance, but that wasn't how it worked out. The instant her eyes caught sight of him, she did a little mental exploring.

His well-worn jeans rested on his hips and fit snugly over his thighs. He had some sort of tool belt around his waist, and even though there was a slight chill in the air, he was wearing just a shabby gray T-shirt with a few splatters of pink paint on it. By the time her eyes met his, Emma's mouth was bone dry and her pulse was pounding in her head.

"Good morning," she said in a relatively normal voice.

"Morning," he replied over the sound of David thundering down the stairs.

"Hey," David greeted Sam.

"Hey," she answered back.

There was an awkward teenage moment before David said, "C'mon up to my room; we can work there."

"Like hell," Conner interjected. "You'll work down here at the kitchen table."

"Dad!" Sam whined. "You'll be making all sorts of noise with your saw and whatever else. We need to have quiet."

"I don't like the idea," Conner said.

"They'll be fine," Emma promised. "Sam, would you like some coffee?"

"Yes, please."

Jeanine interjected, "I'll be upstairs with them. Sheriff, I promise nothing but studying will come of this."

Conner's shoulders slumped as he relented. "In that case, okay." Then he turned to Emma. "Do I get coffee, too?"

"Sure."

"I've got to bring some stuff in from my truck," he explained.

"Need help?" she asked.

He shook his head. "Coffee is enough."

When he turned to go out the door Emma was treated to an unobstructed view of his back. Broad shoulders tapered to slim hips, and then he had that hot backside that made her warm in places she hadn't even known she had. "Coffee is so not enough," she muttered as she made him a steaming mug.

The kids and their watchdog went upstairs, and Emma found herself studying Conner through the kitchen window. He set-up two saw horses, then took a length of wood and started sawing. Sometimes, when he moved, the fabric of his shirt pulled taut against his stomach and she could make out the outlines of a very well-defined torso. And his arms were massive. For just a brief second she wondered what it might feel like to have him wrap those arms around her.

"Dangerous detour," she warned herself. But that didn't stop her from looking her fill.

When Conner returned, he took a measuring tape out of his toolbelt. "This shouldn't take long."

"Have your coffee first," she said. "Before it gets cold."

He paused for a millisecond, then joined her at the table tucked under the window. They sat across from each another at the table. "Cream? Sugar?"

He shook his head. "Black works."

"Have you recovered from the party?" she asked, hoping to keep it light so her hormones would settle down.

He shrugged. "I have to run for re-election every four years, so I'm pretty used to sucking up to the town council."

"You don't impress me as a suck-up."

"You've never seen me shake babies and kiss hands."

She laughed. "Isn't that supposed to be the other way around?"

His gray eyes glinted with good humor. "Fifty-fifty."

Emma slid the plate of sweet rolls in his direction. "Have one. Jeanine made them and they are *amazing*."

He took a bite and agreed. "Really good. You can't cook?"

"I can cook," Emma defended herself. "I'm not The Ghost of Julia Child or anything, but I get by."

"Then why hire Jeanine?"

"Just because I *can* cook doesn't mean I *like* to cook."

Conner took a napkin from the holder in the center of the table and wiped his hands. "Time to get to work," he announced as he stood. He went over to the trash can to get rid of the napkin but as soon as he opened the lid, Emma winced.

"What the hell is this?" he asked, plucking the limp, bloody tulip from the top of the trash.

She waved her hand. "It's nothing. A prank, like you said."

"Where was it?"

"On the front door mat when I got home last night."

"Why didn't you call me?"

She sighed heavily. "Because there wasn't anything you could have done."

"First someone shooting out your window casing, and now *this*?" All signs of humor faded. A nerve pulsed in his jaw. "I'll post a deputy here."

"No," she insisted. "I'm having a state-of-the-art security system put in tomorrow. Complete with cameras and motion sensors."

"That's a good idea."

"See?" she said with her arms out, palms up. "Problem solved. If anyone creeps up on my porch again, I'll light them up like a Christmas tree and take their photo. Then I'll call you."

He reached into his back pocket, took a card out of his wallet, then used the pencil he had tucked behind his ear and scribbled something on the back. He handed it to her.

"This is my cell number. Call me if something like this happens again."

"I'm kind of hoping it won't. It's kind of creepy."

"And you're sure you haven't made any enemies in Purdue?"

She rose but she still had to crane her neck to meet his gaze. "Of course I'm sure. I mean Whitley didn't like me taking over his cases. Hayden doesn't like losing and your deputies don't like being bested in court, but I hardly think any of them would behave so childishly. So far the only person I seem to personally irritate is you."

He took a step closer so they were barely a breath apart. "I'm not irritated. I'm interested."

Her belly flip-flopped. She felt the warmth of his breath on her upturned face. All she had to do was reach out and draw him in. But that was far more dangerous than a few bloody flowers on her front porch. "You don't know anything about me," she said with a slight catch in her throat.

"I'd like to change that," he said, dipping his head.

Emma was rigid until she felt him snake his arm around her back as his lips gently explored hers. He nibbled her lower lip and then slipped his tongue inside her mouth.

Because of her better angels, Emma flattened her palms against his rock-solid chest. The plan had been to push him away but that thought went out of her head as soon as she touched him. Her head was literally spinning and it took some self-control to keep from lifting the hem of his shirt so she could explore skin to skin.

He moaned against her mouth and she felt the sound coursing through her. Then he slowly pulled back, raising his hands to cup her face. His eyes searched hers. He offered a cocky half-smile. "You didn't slap me."

"Yet."

CHAPTER TWELVE

A week had passed since Emma had last seen Conner. Well, that wasn't exactly true: They'd passed one another at the courthouse a few times but he'd done little more than tip his hat in her direction.

Of course she couldn't decipher a hat tip. Did that mean *great kiss* or *that kiss was so bad I've decided to join the clergy*? Still, she understood avoidance and Conner was definitely avoiding her. And she was returning the favor. Emma stayed late at the office every night, ensuring she'd miss Conner when he came to pick up Sam after her tutoring sessions.

She sighed heavily and went back to the pile of folders on her desk. Thanks to the long hours, she was completely caught up and was considering going out for a bite for dinner when she heard a noise.

Looking up, she saw Conner standing in her doorway. Hatless, he wore his uniform and a broad grin. "Evening," he greeted her.

"Hi." It suddenly seemed difficult for her to breathe normally, so the word came out sounding sultry and embarrassingly alluring.

His answer started with a sexy half-smile. "I'm here on a mission."

"Mumm-humm." She didn't trust her voice. Not when he looked so good in his uniform. "I'm supposed to take you out to dinner."

Blinking, she looked up at him. "What?"

"Jeanine told Mary that you rarely eat dinner. Mary told George—he's the gardener for the Burkes—who told Stella, who told me."

"I thought you didn't get involved with gossip."

"I'm making an exception this time. Grab your purse and let's get out of here."

"I have work to do," she protested.

"You're probably ahead of your workload. C'mon, Emma. Live dangerously."

She took her purse and briefcase out of the bottom drawer of her desk, then took another minute to freshen her lipstick. "Stella's or the rib place—which makes an amazing Cobb salad."

He chuckled. "Who orders a salad from a rib joint?" He shifted his weight to one leg and leaned into the jam. "There's a decent seafood place two counties over. Game?"

She tilted her head. "Are you asking me out on a date?"

"I never used the word 'date.' "

"But what you described sure sounds like a date."

He sighed. "Okay, yes. I'm inviting you to dinner."

"See? Was that so hard?" Emma asked smugly. She stood and gathered her purse and her briefcase.

"Actually, yes."

* * *

She went to pass him and he grabbed her arm. She looked up and their eyes locked. Then ever so slowly, he dipped his head and brushed his warm lips against hers. He could feel her tense at first, then relax as he deepened the kiss. It was a good thing he'd wrapped his arms around her because she relaxed in his grip.

He could feel the heat of her body through the thin fabric of her blouse; he could feel the contours of her waist before his hand moved lower and gave her firm butt a gentle squeeze. His tongue sparred with hers and he could taste her uneven breathing. Conner had expected a reaction, but not to this degree. Knowing how much she wanted him stroked his ego, among other things.

But then he allowed his past to creep in. His first wife, Lisa, had kept up the pretext of their marriage all while she was having an affair with her boss. He didn't know enough about Emma to even think about trusting her yet.

He gently set her away and smiled down at her flustered face. "This could get addictive," he said, reluctantly dropping his hands to his sides.

"Yes…well…What about dinner?" Emma glanced down at her wrist. "It's after nine."

"We can make it. Shrimpers stays open until eleven."

"And no one will see us there?" she asked.

He shook his head and his smile broadened. "Don't worry. No wagging tongues will know I took the new girl to dinner."

"New girl?" she repeated, lips pursed.

He shrugged. "It's not a terrible nickname."

"What about calling me by my name?"

"What's the fun in that? We'll take my car," he said as they approached the elevator.

"Won't someone see us?"

"Most of Purdue rolls up for the night by nine."

* * *

After a nearly silent forty-minute drive, Conner parked his SUV in the nearly empty lot of the restaurant. The décor was definitely fishing—nets, sea shells and walls littered with photos. Some poor departed fish covered the walls, along with some buoys and other fishing-themed things.

"What is that smell?" she whispered.

"Garlic cheese biscuits," he answered. "I could make a meal out of them."

"They're making me salivate."

Conner placed his hand at the small of her back as the hostess showed them to a booth near the rear of the dining room. There were only two other couples in the restaurant and one guy in a floppy fishing hat seated at the bar nursing his drink.

A middle-aged woman greeted Conner with familiarity,

then offered Emma a warm smile. "What can I get you two to drink?"

"I'll take a beer," Conner said.

"Same here," Emma said as she was handed a menu. "So, what's good here?"

"Everything," he answered. "The salmon is brought in fresh daily. Sam orders it every time I bring her here."

"Salmon it is," Emma said as she closed the voluminous menu.

The waitress returned with their beers and took their orders. Soft music fell from speakers mounted in the ceiling. The songs were obviously on a loop because by the time their dinner arrived, Jimmy Buffet was singing "Margaretville" for the second time.

"You were right," she said after she swallowed her first bite of fish. "This is amazing."

"Maybe it just tastes good because you've skipped dinner for the last six days."

She shot him a sidelong glance. "Are my eating habits really the topic of conversation in Purdue?"

"No," he said as he cut the hunk of steak on his plate. "They also talk about you hiring Willis, Jeanine's new car, and the fact that you put in a security system."

"I'm amazed they don't know the code," she teased.

"Give them time," Conner joked.

"This town needs a distraction that *isn't* me."

"Good luck with that."

Emma's fork hovered above her food. "What about you? Ever been the center of town gossip?"

"Yep."

"Care to share?"

He shrugged. "My very private custody battle became very public. For a while there I thought the town would print T-shirts that said 'Team Conner' and 'Team Lisa.'"

"But aren't you a local guy? Wouldn't they automatically side with you?"

"Lisa was also a local."

Emma pushed her plate aside. "Let me guess. You married your high school sweetheart."

"Can we change the subject?"

"Not yet," she said with a twinge of enjoyment. She waved the general shape of a human being. "You were on the football team and she was a cheerleader and I'll bet you were homecoming king and queen. Then you got married young and lived happily ever after."

"Drop it."

"Not until you admit that you were the Ken and Barbie of Purdue High School."

"Fine. Everything you said is true. Except for the part about living happily ever after. I worked a lot and I got my degree online, so I was very rarely focused on our relationship."

"Relationships need nurturing."

"Yeah, well, she did what most women in her position would do."

"Which was?"

"She had an affair with her boss. Fell in love and moved with him to Chicago. Now personally I don't much care where she lives or with whom, but she got primary physical custody of Sam and I don't think that's fair. I have as much right to our daughter as she does."

"When did she get physical custody?"

"Two years ago. And as much as it pains me to say it, Sam's stepfather Barry pays for her to go to a special math and technology school. She has her heart set on MIT."

"Were you chief of police then?" Emma asked.

He shook his head. "Only got promoted eighteen months ago."

"That's a substantial change in circumstances."

He put his knife and fork down, then took a swallow of beer. "I don't follow."

"Custody can be revisited by the court whenever there's a substantial change in circumstances."

"I don't want to take her out of school. I just want her for every school break and alternating Christmases."

"Bring me your divorce papers and I'll get started, but you have to tell Sam about this because at her age, the judge will listen to whatever she says."

"How much is this going to cost me?"

"Pro bono. A way of thanking you for fixing my window casing. Now there's no breeze wafting through the room."

"I thought you were a criminal attorney."

"I still had to take matrimonial law."

"At Harvard?"

"Did Elgin pass around my résumé?"

Conner smiled and it caused a fluttering in her stomach. "Your sweatshirt."

"What?"

"The night I first met you at The Grille. You were wearing a Harvard sweatshirt."

She winced. "Right."

"And you pulled a gun on me."

"It was just a little gun."

He laughed. "I didn't say it was intimidating, just that it was a gun."

"I know how to use it," she assured him. "My sister and I spent many an afternoon shooting cans off a log."

"In New York?"

She shook her head and wondered how to move off this topic without seeming too obvious. "Georgia."

"And your sister?"

"Amelia."

"Any other family?"

"My mother, but she's in poor health."

"Then why come to Purdue? Shouldn't you have gone back to Georgia to be with her?"

Of course. But she asked me to do this once I told her about the clippings. "Amelia has it covered for now."

"Older or younger sister?"

"Technically I'm the oldest."

He rubbed the stubble starting to show on his chin. "Technically?"

"We're twins."

"There's two of you?"

"Hardly. Amelia is a worrier and I'm more proactive." Emma shifted in her seat. "What about you? Siblings?"

"You know about Michael," he said in a pained tone. "Then there's Declan and Jack. They're both down in Palm Beach County but they'll be here next week for Michael's parole hearing."

"Where do you fit in the birth order?"

"I'm the second from the top."

"Are you all close?"

He nodded. "Thick as thieves."

The waitress appeared to offer them dessert. They declined, then Conner asked, "Do you mind stopping by my house on the way back to your car? I promised Sam I'd bring her some book on Western Civilization she wants David to read."

Emma smiled. "You just said his name without sarcasm dripping off each syllable. You're coming around."

"Yeah, well, I'm not all the way there yet."

* * *

Since Emma hadn't really wondered what his home might be like, she was intrigued by its simplicity. It was a modest, single-story stucco home with Spanish barrel roof tiles. The house was peach and the tiles were rust, so it looked very "Florida." Inside the front door was a modest foyer, then the room opened to a combination living room/dining room. Off to the right was a functional, if dated, kitchen. The furnishings were mostly mismatched but somehow it worked.

As soon as she reached the family room, Conner drew her into his embrace. He kissed her hard, then lifted her up and silently carried her to his bedroom. He slowly undid the buttons on her blouse, revealing her lacy demi-bra. He did the same with her skirt, until she was wearing nothing save for her undergarments. His eyes were smoldering in the moonlight and Emma was smoldering as well. Every nerve ending was on fire and she wanted him desperately.

Conner seemed to be taking his time and reveling it. He even took his time undressing.

Emma flattened her hands against his chest, enjoying the strong beat of his heart beneath her touch.

Her eyes roamed boldly over the vast expanse of his broad shoulders, drinking in the sight of his impressive upper body. She openly admired his powerful thighs and washboard-perfect abs. "Whenever we're together, my self-control seems to go right out the window." She looked up at him, enjoying the anticipation fluttering in her stomach.

Protected in the circle of his arms, Emma closed her eyes and allowed her cheek to rest against his chest. It would be wonderful to forget why she was here in Purdue. Just for a little while. To pretend she was the woman he loved instead of the woman who'd deceived him from the get-go. To forget everything but the magic of being with him.

His fingers danced over her spine, leaving a trail of electrifying sensation in their wake as he removed the rest of her clothing. Passion blossomed and flourished from deep within her, filling her quickly with a frenzied desire he conjured with every touch. Every glance. He ignited feelings so powerful and so intense that Emma fleetingly wondered if this was some sort of out-of-body experience. Then he moved the tip of his finger across her taut nipple and for a split second she couldn't think, except maybe to consider begging when he stopped.

* * *

Conner moved his hand in slow, sensual circles until it rested against her ribcage, just under the swell of her breast. He wanted to see the desire in her eyes. Catching her chin between his thumb and forefinger, he tilted her head up with the intention of searching her eyes. He never made it that far.

His eyes were riveted to her lips, which were slightly parted, a glistening shade of pale rose. His eyes roamed over every feature and he could feel her pulse rate increasing.

Lowering his head, he took a tentative taste. Her mouth was warm and pliant; so was her body, which again pressed urgently against him. His hands roamed purposefully, memorizing every nuance and curve.

He felt his own body respond with an ache, then an almost overwhelming rush of desire surged through him. Her arms slid around his waist, pulling him closer. Conner marveled at the perfect way they fit together. It was as if Emma had been made for him. For this.

"Emma," he whispered against her mouth. He toyed with a lock of her hair first, then slowly wound his hand through the silken mass and gave a gentle tug, forcing her head back even more. Looking down at her face, Conner knew there was no other sight on earth as beautiful and inviting as her blue eyes.

Her long hair fanned out against the pillow case. With a single finger, Conner reached out to trace the delicate outline of her mouth. Her skin had a faint, rosy flush.

He began showering her face and neck with light kisses. His mouth searched for that sensitive spot at the base of her throat. A pleasurable moan spilled from his mouth when she began running her palms over the tight muscles of his stomach.

He kissed her for a long time, savoring the slower pace and the minty taste of her.

Capturing both of her hands in one of his, Conner gently held them above her head. The position arched her back, drawing his eyes down to the outline of her erect nipples.

"This isn't playing fair."

"Believe me, Emma, it's better for both of us if I don't let you keep touching me," he reassured her with a smile and a kiss.

Emma responded by lifting her body to him. The rounded swell of one exposed breast brushed his arm. His fingers closed over the rounded fullness.

"Please let me touch you!" Emma cried out.

"Not yet," he whispered as he ignored her futile struggle to release her hands. He dipped his head to kiss the raging pulse point at her throat. Her soft skin grew hot as he worked his mouth lower and lower. She gasped when his mouth closed around her nipple, then called his name in a hoarse voice that caused a tremor to run the full length of his body.

Moments later he lifted his head, only long enough to see her passion-filled expression and to tell her she was beautiful.

"So are you."

Whether it was the sound of her voice or possibly the way she pressed herself against him, Conner neither knew nor cared. He found himself nearly undone by the level of passion communicated by the movements of her supple body.

He sought her mouth again as he released his hold on her hands and his body moved to cover hers, and his tongue thrust deeply into the warm recesses of her mouth. He moved one hand downward, skimming the side of her body all the way to her thigh. Then, giving in to the urgent need pulsing through him, Conner positioned himself between her legs. Every muscle in his body tensed as he looked at her face before directing his attention lower, to the point where they would join.

Emma lifted her hips, welcoming, inviting, as her hands fell to his hips and she tugged him toward her.

"You're amazing," he groaned against her lips.

"Thank you," she whispered back. "I want you. Now, please?"

He wasted no time responding to her request. In a single motion, he thrust deeply inside of her, knowing without question that he had found heaven on earth.

The sheer pleasure of being inside of her sweet softness was very powerful. He kept the rhythm of their lovemaking at a slow, deliberate pace, enjoying each time he felt the small shivers of her body convulsing. He treated her to a series of slow, building climaxes.

A long, pleasurable time later, Emma again wrapped her legs around his hips just as explosive waves surged from him. One after the other, ripples of pleasure poured from him into her. Satisfaction had never been so powerful.

With his head nestled next to hers, the sweet scent of her hair filled his nostrils. Conner reluctantly relinquished possession of her body. It took several minutes before his breathing slowed to a steady, satiated pace.

Rolling onto his side next to her, Conner rested his head against his arm and gazed down at her. She was sheer perfection. He could have happily stayed next to her in the big, soft bed until the end of time.

"So, tell me more about you," he said.

Her lashes fluttered against her cheeks and he sensed a sudden change. A definite chill that stabbed him right in the gut.

Then her cell phone chirped.

CHAPTER THIRTEEN

She's here?" Emma sat up in bed and reflexively covered herself with the sheet, cell phone in hand as she listened to Jeanine.

"She who?" Conner asked.

She covered the mouthpiece. "My sister."

He kissed the top of her head. "Then we'd better get you home. Besides, I was supposed to pick Sam up thirty minutes ago."

Once they were dressed they started for the door, where Conner stopped her and wrapped his arms around her. "One last time." His mouth closed over hers.

It was a knee-melting kiss that seared her nerve endings. Emma's stomach fluttered and a strong sense of need filled her belly and threatened to send her crashing to the floor.

While the kiss made her toes curl and her heart pound, Emma was distracted by a mantra reminding her that this wasn't going to go anywhere. Once he found out who she really was, he'd probably run. Fast.

She really didn't know enough about him yet. But it was impossible to be objective when just a kiss rendered her stupid.

Like a couple of teenagers who had snuck out the basement window, Emma suggested that Conner drop her off at the municipal parking garage and head to her house first. She promised she'd be right behind him.

"Or"—wicked delight sparkled in his eyes—"we could just say we had dinner together."

"For two hours?"

He shrugged. "I don't think anyone was timing us."

Emma tilted her head to look up into his eyes. "I don't want to give the town gossips any more ammunition."

He smiled. "I see your point. Though it does make me look good, scoring dinner with you and all."

She jokingly elbowed him in the ribcage. "I'm serious. I don't want to be fodder for the grist mill. Especially not now that Amelia is in town."

"How does Amelia play into this?"

Emma couldn't tell him the truth without revealing her own secrets.

"Twins are a freak show," she said evasively.

"Are you identical?" he asked.

Emma nodded. "Except for our choices when it comes to fashion. Amelia is very Bohemian. She has more piercings than I can keep track of."

"But hair, face…"

"The same. Why?"

"Just curious."

She rolled her eyes. "Please tell me you aren't one of those freaks with a twin threesome fantasy?"

"Never," he said earnestly. "I just can't picture you having a duplicate."

"That's just the physical part of it. Amelia and I are as different as night and day."

"How so?" he asked as he finished buttoned his uniform shirt.

"I've wanted to be an attorney since I was eleven. Harvard was my dream. Amelia drifted from community college to community college, taking mostly pottery classes, until she got bored and dropped out completely. Don't get me wrong; she's a great potter, but it's hard to make a living doing arts and crafts shows."

"We have an arts and crafts show in about a week. I'm sure she could set up a table and—"

"I don't think she'll be here that long. As I said, my mother is quite ill."

"Sorry to hear that. What's wrong with her?" he asked.

"She suffered a stroke a few months ago, and it's been downhill since then. Two weeks ago she had a heart attack, so things don't look good."

Conner held her gaze. "Two weeks ago? That's about when you moved to Purdue. Why didn't you go to her side instead of taking an out-of-state job?"

"I'm supporting my mother and supplementing my sister."

"But since you have more money than Renac Burke, you don't have to work."

They were entering dangerous territory. "My mother insisted I take the job." That was true enough.

"So why is your sister here?"

Emma shrugged. "Probably to chew me out. She's a little annoyed with me."

Luckily they'd arrived at her car, effectively ending the conversation. Then the awkwardness set in again. The console between them in Conner's SUV included a computer and a radio system, and it was effectively keeping them apart. Tension crackled in the air. He was looking at her mouth and she was looking at his. Her stomach knotted but she didn't know whether to lean in for another kiss—which she wanted more than her next breath—or simply to step out of the SUV with a belly full of desire.

Conner made the decision for her. "See ya in a few minutes."

"Right." Emma did her best to dismount from the high-profile vehicle. The sound of her heels hitting concrete echoed through the nearly deserted garage. Pressing her key fob, she heard the Mercedes chirp loudly and its lights flashed.

Once she was alone with her thoughts, she realized that having sex with Conner had been stupid. It was a complication piled on a whole case of complications. She had to find out who had been sending the clippings and why. That was the goal. Not sleeping with the hottest guy in town.

She groaned as she pressed the start button for her engine. *And now I get to go home and deal with a presumably pissed Amelia.*

Her driveway was crowded with vehicles. She assumed the red mid-size she didn't recognize was Amelia's rental. She was relieved that Jeanine, David, Conner, and Sam were in the house. That would keep Amelia silent. There was no way her sister would discuss the news clippings or Emma's presence in Purdue in front of strangers. So for now Emma figured she'd have a brief reprieve.

As soon as she stepped inside she smelled coffee and heard the din of conversation in the living room. Plastering a smile on her face, she dropped her purse on the front table and joined the group.

Jeanine leapt up and asked, "Would you like something to eat?"

"Thanks, I ate earlier, but coffee would be great." Emma made a beeline for her sister and gave her a hug. She could feel several pairs of eyes on her. On *them*, actually.

"You look wonderful," she told Amelia as she took a step back. Her sister was wearing a cute, Bohemian-style short dress with leggings and a pair of ballet flats. Her ears, nose, and eyebrow were pierced, and large hoop earrings dangled to her shoulders.

"You look tired," Amelia observed. She checked a funky plastic watch on her wrist. "Do you always work this late?"

Emma shrugged. "I went out to dinner after work. I would have come straight home had I known you were coming."

Amelia smiled. "Had you known, you'd only have blown me off."

That was true. "How is Mom?"

"The same," Amelia said sadly.

"Hey, Sam?" Conner interjected. "Get your stuff. We need to leave these ladies alone to catch up."

"Right," Sam said. Then she handed David a book and told him what chapter to read. David only nodded but Emma read a little more into his gesture than that. If she had to guess, she'd say David was smitten with his attractive tutor. She glanced over at Conner, but if he noticed anything he didn't let on—which told her he hadn't noticed that his baby girl had an admirer.

With the Kavanaughs gone after a few moments, Jeanine and David excused themselves as well and Emma finally found herself alone with her sister. Amelia wasted no time getting to the point of her surprise visit. "You've been here for two weeks and unless you're hiding something from me, you don't know anything more than you did before coming to this place."

"I'm still getting the lay of the land," Emma insisted. "It isn't like I can just walk up to people and ask them if they know anything that would explain why our father assassinated a sitting president."

Amelia sighed loudly. "The *why* doesn't matter, Em. We've known that since we were kids. Mom went to a lot of trouble to shield us from the public. New names, new location, a normal life. You're putting all that at risk."

Emma took a sip of coffee. "Does this mean you

still haven't told your fiancé our dirty little secret?"

Blushing slightly, Amelia nodded. "I'm marrying a wonderful man with a large extended family. I don't want them to know that my father was a killer. Would you?"

Shrugging, Emma thought about it for a minute. "I think I'd have to tell the truth. Like it or not, that is our history."

"No, our history is what Mom did afterward. I'd much rather tell people I was raised by a single mother after the untimely accidental death of my father when I was eleven. That's normal. A hell of a lot more normal than 'I'm the assassin's daughter.' I'd think you would understand that. Look what happened to you in New York." Amelia said.

"I know. But you have to understand that I have to do this. Someone in this town knows who I am and they went to a lot of trouble to get me here. I want to know why." Emma argued.

Amelia huffed. "Just to screw with you?"

"Then why not send the clippings to you or to Mom? Why me and why now?" Emma asked.

Amelia frowned and asked, "Does it really matter?"

"That someone knows the truth?" Amelia parroted. "Yes."

"I agree, which is why I plan on staying here until I find out the who and the why."

"Have you learned anything so far?" Amelia asked.

"I met Kenny Simms." Amelia gave her a blank stare. "He was the police officer who shot Daddy," Emma added.

Amelia's eyes grew wide. "How did you meet him?"

"We were introduced at a party. I've also met most of the

movers and shakers in Purdue's political landscape. And my housekeeper is a virtual font of information."

"She seems nice."

"Jeanine is wonderful. Her son David has potential, too."

Amelia laughed. "You always were one to pick up strays. Is everyone on your payroll?"

"No, just Jeanine and Willis Maddox. He's working on the grounds around the house."

"This house you have alarmed to the teeth?" her sister asked, with one brow arched accusingly.

"I live out in the sticks. It's prudent."

"You have a conceal-and-carry permit. God help anyone who would try to break in to this place." Amelia's expression grew serious. "Unless something has already happened…"

"Not really. Nothing that can't be explained away simply. Besides, the town sheriff is here twice a day to drop off his daughter and pick her up again."

Amelia smiled slyly. "The hot sheriff?"

Emma felt her face grow warm.

"Oh my God! You're blushing. You're sleeping with him."

"Amelia! We're just acquaintances."

"With benefits."

The warmth grew into a raging inferno. "We're consenting adults."

"That was fast."

"Too fast," Emma agreed. "I'm going to put the brakes on it. The last thing I need is a distraction."

"You need to come home," Amelia said with conviction.

"There's nothing here that can lead to anything good. Well, except for Sheriff Kavanaugh."

"Please stop saying that." Emma stood. "I'm exhausted and I have to work tomorrow. I hope you don't mind sharing. I gave the guest rooms to David and Jeanine."

"I have a reservation at the airport Hilton. I have an early flight out in the morning."

"You just dropped in for a few minutes?"

"I wanted to beg you to come home in person but I can see you've dug your heels in. Please, Em, don't do anything that dredges up the past."

"No promises," she replied apologetically. "I'm sorry."

Amelia grabbed her purse. "I also wanted to tell you that Mom signed a DNR."

Emma felt the implications of that stab her in the heart. "When did she do that?"

"A year ago. When she was diagnosed with high blood pressure. It was on file with her general practitioner and he sent it over to the critical care unit."

Emma sucked in a breath and shook her head. "Damn it."

"I just thought you should know."

"Thanks." Emma moved to hug her sister. "And thank you for taking care of Mom while I do this."

"I wish you wouldn't. Can't you let this alone?" Amelia practically pleaded.

"No," she answered quietly. "Do you know how to get back to the airport?"

Amelia nodded. "Think about what I've said, Em. I'll call you tomorrow when I get home."

"Love you."

"Love you, too."

She watched from the window as Amelia drove off. Thoughts pinged around in her brain. Knowing her mother had lost the will to live. Knowing how much her decision to come to Purdue was aggravating Amelia. Then from time to time thoughts about Conner seeped in, reigniting her desire.

She showered and went to bed but sleep was elusive. She was tossed and turned. She tried reading. Nothing seemed to work.

Then the quiet of the house was shattered by the shrill ring of the phone.

"Hello?" she said as she grabbed it before the first ring ended, fully expecting it to be news about her mother.

"Emma, it's Conner."

She looked at the bedside clock. "It's two in the morning."

"I'm at the hospital."

"Are you okay?"

"Yes. It isn't—"

"Sam?"

"No, it's your sister."

"Amelia? What happened?" She was already out from under the covers and heading to her closet.

"Close as we can tell, someone ran her off the road."

CHAPTER FOURTEEN

What is it?" Amelia asked as she chased a bit of egg around on her plate. It had been three days since the accident and she was cleared to fly home tomorrow.

Emma slipped her fingernail beneath the envelope's seal and slit it open. "An invitation from Renae Burke for tea."

Amelia rolled her eyes. "You hate tea."

Emma shushed her sister since Jeanine was just steps away in the kitchen. "But I need to know more about Renae and her husband." Emma began to stuff folders into her briefcase. "I want to know what she remembers about that day." She closed her case and grabbed her purse. "I'm sorry Jeanine has to be the one to take you to the airport. I missed the mandatory meeting so now I have a heavy caseload of drunk and disorderlies and one icky child porn addict to represent."

"You do have all the fun," Amelia teased, pushing back her chair and getting to her feet. "I'll walk you out."

ABANDONED 171

"You don't have to do that."

Amelia nodded in Jeanine's direction, then followed Emma out the front door.

The sun was just cresting the horizon and the morning air was damp and fragrant from the scent of some sort of flowers Willis had planted on either side of the staircase. She didn't know flowers, just that these smelled good and were a pretty shade of pink.

"I'm genuinely scared for you," Amelia said on a rush of breath. "What if my accident wasn't an accident?"

"I've seen the way you drive," Emma quipped. "You admitted that you cut someone off just minutes before. That's road rage, dear sister. Not some convoluted conspiracy plot out to kill us both."

Emma was startled when Willis Maddox appeared out of the mist. For a large man, he was very stealthy.

"Keep it up and I'll have to put a bell around your neck, too," Emma joked.

"Ma'am?"

"Nothing," Emma said. "Jeanine has your money for you. Are you going to start on the backyard this week?"

"Yes, ma'am."

"You can call me Emma," she told him for the umpteenth time. She turned back to her sister and gave her a gentle hug, avoiding the sling on her left arm. "Call me when you get home so I won't worry."

"I will."

Emma slipped behind the wheel and headed for her office. She'd put up something of a brave front for her sister. In reality, she was starting to wonder if all these little incidents *were* related and dangerous. If Amelia had actually been run off the road, it could have been because she'd been mistaken for Emma. After all, they both drove red cars and they did look identical to one another.

"What I wouldn't give for a sounding board," she muttered as she pulled into her regular spot in the garage in the municipal building.

She was the first one into the office so she went into the kitchenette and made a pot of coffee before attempting to tackle the stack of files on her desk. As she went back to her office, mug in hand, Harriett was just placing her sweater over the back of her chair. Harriett was a paralegal with the P.D.'s office and Emma was impressed with her work. She was a friendly twentysomething brunette with an eventual goal of going to law school. Emma smiled. "Good morning."

"It is, isn't it?" the other woman replied. "I love springtime. Not too hot yet."

"I've been forewarned about the Florida summer," Emma said ruefully.

"It sucks," the pretty brunette said. "I swore that once I got out of school I was going to move someplace with real seasons."

"But?"

"I ended up with an Associate's degree in Paralegal Sciences and got this job and well, I just stayed will I earned my B.S."

"For which I am eternally grateful," Emma insisted. "You make my life ultimately easier."

Harriett scoffed. "You hardly have me do anything. Mr. Whitley treats me like his personal gofer."

"Bill and I have a different approach to things."

"Yeah," Harriett said in a near-whisper. "You aren't an ass-hole."

Emma was smiling as she returned to her office and began to read. Her smile faded as she read file after file. It seemed as if every young man between the ages of twenty and thirty had spent the weekend literally drunk and disorderly. The only thing that differed between the files was the definition of disorderly: public urination, a brawl at The Grille…even a guy found swimming in the town fountain in his under-wear.

In her experience, these folks sobered up and regretted the error of their ways. But she'd spend the majority of the day in court making that very argument.

Elgin called her into his office just as she was heading over to the courthouse. "How is your sister?" he asked.

Emma stood behind the visitor's chair. "Fine. She's leaving—"

"This morning," he finished.

"Was that in the local paper?"

"No. I've got a nephew who works at the motorcycle shop. David Segan told him. My useless nephew told his mother and my sister-in-law told me."

"I keep forgetting that this town doesn't need a news-paper."

Elgin smiled. "Sorry you got the short stick this week but I warned you about missing the morning meeting."

"I don't mind," she said. "Well. I mind the Charles Lawson case. Any chance you'd give that one to Bill? I'll take a half dozen of his cases in the deal."

"Lawson?" Elgin repeated. "The weather guy, right?"

"He was on the local news channel as a meteorologist until the cops caught him trying to hook up with a fifteen-year-old boy. Then they executed a search warrant on his house and found a ton of kiddy porn on his computer. I hate child molesters."

"I'll see what I can do," Elgin said, then he checked his watch. "You'd better go. Don't want to be late with Judge Crandall."

Emma made her way to the courthouse and greeted people as she was taken to the attorney conference room in the basement of the building. She met with her first client, and as expected, he was contrite.

"It was a bachelor party," he explained. "I vaguely remember someone daring me to swim in the fountain. It was stupid."

"Yes it was," she agreed. "This is your first arrest?" she asked, flipping through the folder.

"Yes ma'am."

"Do you work?"

"I design software. It's entry level and I work out of my home, except when the company needs me. Then I drive to Greenville, North Carolina, for a few days."

"Married?"

"Yes, with two kids."

"Are you the sole supporter of your family?"

"Yes. And my wife isn't working since she had the second baby so I couldn't even afford to bond myself out this weekend."

Emma met his gaze. "Don't worry about that. I'm free, part of the Constitution at work." She paused and offered him a smile. "Given your history and your otherwise exemplary record, I'll ask the prosecutor for probation before judgment."

"What does that mean?"

"It means you'll get probation for a period of time and if you keep your nose clean, the charge will be dismissed."

He sighed heavily. "Thank you."

"Don't thank me yet. I'll see you upstairs." Emma took her things and made a quick trip upstairs, then began searching for Hayden Blackwell. She found him in Judge Crandall's court room.

"Good morning," she greeted him.

"Miss McKinley. You seem out of breath."

"I keep meaning to join a gym, but who has the time? Listen, I'd like to talk to you about Michael Ellison. First case on the docket today?"

"The fountain swimmer," Hayden said as he nodded. "I've got dashboard camera video of the guy being yanked out of the fountain in his underwear."

"It was a bachelor party," she explained. "He's actually a stand-up guy, good job, good provider, no record, not even a traffic ticket."

"And your point is?"

"PBJ," she said on a rush of breath.

"You want me to give a drunk probation before judgment?"

"Exactly. C'mon, Hayden. You know this is a just resolution."

"I know it's a bad precedent to set," he replied.

"No, giving a guy a record when all he did was overdo it at a party sets a bad precedent. He has a wife and two kids to support. And he's very, very contrite."

"Okay."

She felt like celebrating. Then he held up one hand.

"But. He pays a two-hundred-dollar fine."

"One hundred." Hayden gave her a stern glare. "He's an entry level guy with two kids in diapers. Two hundred would be a real hardship."

"Probation for one year including random drug and alcohol testing."

"Done."

Hayden smiled. "Don't you have to run any of this past your client?"

"He'll be thrilled, trust me."

* * *

Her day was long and not nearly over when she returned to her office at five-thirty. Her briefcase was heavy with files and paperwork she needed to complete on all her cases from that day. Ever helpful Harriett was gone, as was everyone except Elgin. He was in his office with the door closed, but she could hear him speaking—just not well enough to make out any words.

After depositing her heavy bag on a chair, she took off her jacket and hung it on the hook on the back of her door. After leaving briefly to make a fresh pot of coffee she returned to face the mound of paperwork, checking her cell phone, expecting a message from her sister. Finding none, she dialed Amelia but the call went to voicemail. She was probably with their mother, Emma decided. There was no cell service in the critical care unit.

Her day had consisted of seven plea bargains and one not-guilty plea. The not guilty had been the perv, who she hoped would become Bill's headache. Until then, not guilty was the only option she could recommend.

Emma was on her fourth case and her fifth cup of coffee when Elgin stuck his head in the door. His tie was loosened and his suit jacket was folded over his arm. "Still here?"

"For a while."

"I'm heading out." He turned, then abruptly turned back. "Bill will take your molester but he's going to dump a half-dozen domestic abusers on you in return."

"Good and fine," she said, relieved. Not that she had a lot of use for domestic violence, but in her world, it was better than arguing in favor of a pervert. "Have a nice evening."

"You too."

Emma went back to her computer and typed out the various terms of the various plea deals. It took her almost an hour to finish. She was standing at the printer when she sensed someone behind her. She glanced back to find Conner Kavanaugh standing by Harriett's desk.

"You scared me," she snapped. "Not very smart to sneak

up on a woman who carries a gun." Which was in her purse, in a locked drawer. In her office. Twenty feet away.

He smiled. "But you keep your gun in your purse, which I'm guessing is in your office. I'd suggest you lock the door if you're going to work alone at night."

"Thanks for the tip." She gathered her documents and went to her office with Conner on her heels. "What do you need?" she asked.

The instant her hands were free, he spun her around and kissed her urgently. Emma's palms were flattened against his chest and she knew the smart thing to do would be to push him away. But she wasn't feeling smart. She was feeling desire. A lot of desire. Toe-curling desire. Her head was spinning so she grabbed his uniform shirt to keep her balance.

Conner deepened the kiss, teasing her tongue with his own as he drew his fingers through her hair. With a gentle tug, he forced her head back a little, then blazed a trail of hot kisses along her throat. Emma couldn't help herself. She moaned, let go of the fabric and allowed her hands to feel the sculpted muscle of his torso through his shirt.

When he took her mouth again, she began to fumble with the buttons. He did the same, only his fingers were far more adept. In no time, he had her blouse pushed back on her shoulders and he was moving her backward until Emma felt the edge of her desk against the back of her thighs. Reflexively, she arched back as Conner lifted his head briefly, then kissed his way to the lacy edge of her bra.

She thought her heart would pound right out of her chest as she continued to undo the buttons on his uniform. Finally, she shoved the shirt open and felt his warm skin against her own. When she moved to his belt, she heard bells chiming,

Momentarily coming out of her sensual fog, she realized the sounds were coming from her cell phone. "I have to get that," she said in a breathy voice she barely recognized.

Conner continued to kiss her neck as she reached behind her and blindly felt around for the phone.

"Hello?"

"Is this Ms. Emma McKinley?"

"Yes."

"This is Helen Jenkins at Mercy Hospital."

She immediately sobered, straightening up and pushing Conner away. "Is it my mother?"

"No," she said. "I was calling about your sister."

"Is she trying to do too much?" Emma asked. That was so like Amelia.

"That's the thing," Helen said. "She called here early this morning and said she'd be here before noon."

"But?"

"She never showed up and she isn't answering her cell phone."

CHAPTER FIFTEEN

Tell me exactly what happened when you took Amelia to the airport," Emma asked Jeanine, hearing the panic in her own voice.

"Well, I drove her to the terminal. I put her bag by the check-in. As I was saying good-bye, she got a call on her cell phone."

"Any idea who it was?" Emma pressed.

Jeanine's eyes grew wide. "I assumed it was you."

Not me. "But she went in to the terminal?"

Jeanine shrugged. "She was on the phone, and you can't park at the curb so I drove off. I'm so sorry."

"It isn't your fault." She turned to Conner. "Can we go look at video at the airport?"

"Sure. C'mon, I'll drive."

"I'll stay here," Sam called from the living room.

Conner looked torn for a second.

"They'll be fine," Emma insisted.

Fear settled in the pit of her stomach while Conner raced down a series of two-lane roads toward the airport.

"Has your sister ever done anything like this before?"

Emma shook her head. "She's flighty when it comes to work but she would never disappear on me. We're close. We tell each other everything."

He gave her a sidelong glance. "Everything?"

Emma shrugged. "She knows we slept together."

Conner shook his head. "And you think news travels fast in Purdue."

"No, I think *gossip* travels fast in Purdue. But I don't care about that now. Now I want to know what happened to my sister."

"Is there anyone she might have called?"

"The hospital where my mother is. Her fiancé, Brody and maybe her friend Regina."

Emma was already pulling her cell out of her purse when Conner suggested, "Give her a call. Maybe she's heard something."

Reggie—as she was known—picked up on the third ring. "Hello?"

"Hi, It's Emma."

"Emma? What a surprise. Is everything okay? Is it your mother?"

"No, she's still about the same. I was wondering when you last spoke to Amelia."

"Early this morning. She was waiting to check-in at the airport."

"How did she seem?"

"Well, glad to be leaving Purdue. But it was a normal call. Nothing jumped out at me; why?"

Emma explained the situation. "I'm on my way to the airport now to check out the video surveillance. Is there any way you could call Brody for me?" They passed a road sign that indicated the airport was just two miles up ahead.

"I'm on it. I'll call you once I speak to him but will you keep me posted?"

"Yes, of course."

Moments later, Conner pulled up and parked his official SUV in the fire lane. Emma was out of the car the minute it came to a full stop. North Central Airport was a modest building, an air traffic control tower, and six runways. Only a few airlines serviced the area, so Emma thought that should make their job easier.

Conner went up to the first officer he saw and flashed his badge, and then they were escorted to the far end of the terminal, to a door marked PRIVATE.

They found themselves in a large room with a wall of monitors covering everything from the parking garage to the tarmac. A short, rotund man came over and extended his hand to Conner. "Lieutenant Tate," he introduced himself. "I'm chief of operations. What can I do for you?"

Conner explained the situation, ending his explanation with, "So, the last time anyone saw her she was at curbside check-in at approximately eight-thirty this morning."

Tate took them into a darkened room with two chairs and a computer. The smell of stale coffee battled with the scent of Tate's cheap cologne. Without pulling out the chair,

Tate leaned over and typed something on the keyboard, then had Conner repeat the time in question. "I've set it up to start playing at eight-fifteen this morning. This arrow plays the footage in real time. This one"—he paused and moved the mouse over a double arrow—"puts it into slow motion."

"Can I do a screen grab?" Emma asked.

"Sure." Tate stepped back and went to the door. "Come find me if you need anything else."

Eyes glued to the screen, Emma sat in front of the computer with Conner to her right. It didn't take but a few minutes for Jeanine's car to come into view.

"There she is. With her bag," Emma narrated. "She's walking up to check-in. Now she's on the phone."

"Then she stops," Conner continued. "Seems to me like she's looking around. Now she's moving away from check-in and farther down the curbside."

Emma was still glued to the screen. "She's off the phone and seems to be looking around."

"For what?" Conner asked rhetorically.

"There's no sound," Emma groaned. She blew out an impatient breath as she watched her sister stand on the curb for nearly ten minutes. "She's taking out her phone again."

"Incoming call," Conner observed.

They watched in silence while Amelia ended the call and a few minutes later a black car pulled up to the curb.

"Freeze that," Conner said. He took a pen and small pad out of his shirt pocket. "Is that last number on the license plate a three or an eight?"

"A three," she said confidently. "Do you know what kind of car that is?"

"Crown Victoria," he told her. "Newer model."

Amelia leaned toward the passenger window, then the trunk popped open and Amelia went around to the back of the car and placed her bag in the trunk and shut it. She went back to the passenger door and got into the car. The entire scene took less than two minutes.

"Any ideas on who that was?" Conner asked.

"Amelia doesn't know anyone in Purdue. I have no idea who that was or why she willingly got into his car."

Conner raked his fingers through his thick, ebony hair. One strand refused to cooperate and before she thought about it, Emma reached out and tucked it into place. Doing so felt intimate and strange all at once. She chalked it up to concern and confusion.

"Is she trusting?" he asked.

Emma nodded. "She can be a little naive when it comes to reading people, but I don't think she'd be careless here."

"Here?" Conner pressed.

"Purdue," she answered solemnly.

"Care to expand on that?"

This was a definite crossroad. She needed his help but telling him the truth was a risk. But with Amelia missing, she didn't feel as if she had a choice.

"Can you run that license plate?"

"The minute we get back to my car." He tucked his finger beneath her chin and lifted her face so he could hold her gaze. "There's something you're not telling me."

"I know."

He frowned. "I'm not looking for affirmation; I'm looking for the truth."

"Which I will tell you when we aren't in an airport security cubicle."

His hand moved so that his palm cupped the side of her face. "I care about you. You can trust me. The last thing I want between us is secrets. That's what destroyed my marriage."

I care about you? What did that mean? And if he thought his marriage had been destroyed by secrets, she was about to unload a real whopper on him.

They thanked Tate and walked out with a screen shot of the license plate of the Crown Vic Amelia was last seen getting into. As soon as they were back in the SUV, Conner leaned over the console and gave her a kiss—a deep, gentle kiss unlike the passionate ones she'd grown to enjoy. It didn't last long but it made a lasting impression. "The license plate?" she prompted.

Conner got on the radio and called in the plate. In a few minutes the radio crackled back to life. "Go ahead," Conner said into the mouthpiece.

"Came back as stolen off a green Celica last night."

"Damn it," Conner groaned. He signed off the radio. "I can pull a list of all the black Crown Vics in the county but it'll be a long list."

"What about her cell phone records?"

Conner nodded. "I can open a missing/endangered case and get a subpoena tonight."

Emma reached out reflexively and squeezed this arm. "You'd do that for me?"

"In case you haven't noticed, there's very little I wouldn't do for you." He reached out and gently placed his hand behind her neck and pulled her closer. This kiss definitely wasn't gentle. This one was powerful enough to make her forget her troubles for a few glorious minutes. And even though he was barely touching her, she felt a jolt of desire course through her with every thrust of his masterful tongue.

Slowly, and with regret in his dark, hooded eyes, Conner let his arm fall away. "Until you, I never thought I'd want to be close to a woman again."

She froze, half from happiness and half from abject fear. "Maybe it's just lust," she said, trying to lighten the mood.

"Don't freak out on me. I'm just letting you know where I stand with this situation. My interest is piqued. But no pressure."

"Definite pressure," she said under her breath. She thought about their situation and realized he wasn't far off the mark. Never in her life had she slept with a man on the first date. And if they hadn't been interrupted by that phone call, she would have made love to him on her office desk earlier. But it was more than the sex. She liked him. Found him easy to be around. Loved his daughter. Weren't those the signs of falling for a guy? God, her dating history was so poorly lacking that she had to make a mental pro/con list. And of course there was one big con: she wasn't really Emma McKinley.

"So you were going to tell me about why your sister would want to get as far away from Purdue as possible."

Now if she told him the whole story he'd probably head for the hills. She'd be putting herself in the same category as his cheating, lying ex-wife. She'd lose *this*. *Him.*

"Can we save that for tomorrow?" she asked. "I'm physically and emotionally exhausted and worried sick about Amelia."

"Sure," he said easily. "I'll take you home, then swing by the office and work on getting your sister's cell records."

"Sam is still at my place," she reminded him. In the dim light from the dashboard she watched him frown. "The tutoring is going well."

"So is the constant texting," he groused, his frown deepening. "I think my daughter might be getting a little too close to your delinquent."

"David is not a delinquent. He's smart and he's a whiz on the computer."

"I know. Sam mentioned that."

"He's very well read and he hasn't done anything wrong since the change in his environment."

"I know. Sam mentioned that, too."

Emma smiled. "You just don't like him."

"I know. I mentioned that to Sam."

"Not to interject myself into your relationship with your daughter but trashing the guy a girl likes usually only makes her like him more."

"Says the woman who doesn't have any kids."

"Says the woman who was once a sixteen-year-old girl."

They reached her driveway, but before he let her get out of the car Conner said, "I have my custody papers in the car."

"Let me have them."

He shook his head. "You have too much on your plate right now."

"Which means I probably won't sleep much, so hand them over."

He reached behind her and dragged up an accordion file. "The divorce from hell," he said, presenting her with the heavy file.

"I'm sure it will be interesting reading and I'll—"

"Will you look at that!" Conner fumed.

Emma followed his gaze and saw the silhouettes of Sam and David in the window. "I guess tutoring is over," she teased.

Conner was not amused. "She's just a kid."

"No, she's a young lady."

"I thought you said Jeanine would chaperone."

"Don't bark at me," Emma told him. "And if you're smart, you won't bark at your daughter either. They're kissing, Conner, not running naked through the house."

His knuckles on the steering wheel went white from his death grip. "She's too young for this. And he's a loser."

"First, she isn't too young to be kissed and second, I'm sure part of David's appeal is his bad boy image. Very powerful stuff to a sixteen-year-old girl. We all have at least one bad boy in our history. It's a rite of passage."

"Please tell me your father kicked the kid's ass."

"My father died when I was eleven." It was the first time

she'd ever said that to anyone. It was oddly freeing. And one small chunk of her real past was revealed. It was a start.

Conner took her hand and brought it to his lips for a kiss. "I'm sorry. I didn't know."

Emma reclaimed her hand. "There's a lot about me you don't know."

"True, but that still doesn't deter my interest."

"If I remember correctly, we first caught sight of each other in a bar where you instigated a fight and I threatened you with my gun."

He smiled broadly. "And what's not to love about that?"

CHAPTER SIXTEEN

Emma had insisted Jeanine go to bed over an hour ago. Guilt had the woman hovering, which made Emma feel more anxious. The only thing that kept her sane was knowing that Amelia had gotten into a car willingly, so maybe there was some harmless explanation for her disappearance.

It was nearly midnight when her restlessness had her jogging out to the mailbox to collect her mail. She figured so long as she stayed busy, the better. She also played it safe, tucking her twenty-two into the waistband of her jeans before heading outside.

Thanks to the newly installed, motion detector lighting Willis had installed, her entire path was illuminated. But when she got to the box, she reached into its dark interior and immediately touched wet *something*. Yanking her hand back, she stared down at the red smear on her palm and swallowed her fear. Cautiously, she took her cell phone out of her pocket and used the flashlight app to light the interior of the mailbox. Lying atop a small stack of mail was another blood-dipped flower.

"Whoever you are," Emma projected her voice as she would do in the courtroom, "You're a fucking, miserable coward! Show yourself. Tell me to my face what the hell your problem is. If this is supposed to be a message, I don't understand it. Too subtle for me, pal. I'm not going to waste my time trying to figure it out. Might as well use your damned words and tell me straight out."

She was met with silence. "Dickhead." Carefully, Emma took everything out of the box and glanced around nervously before jogging back to the house. The minute she was inside she pressed the buttons on the alarm's keypad to arm the house. However, in her frazzled state she ended up making a mistake, and suddenly every light in the house came on and a loud alarm blared. Emma got a grip on herself and was able to hit the kill code just as her landline rang.

"Hello?" she said into the receiver. The echo of the alarm was still reverberating in her head.

"This is Travis at the com center. We're showing an active alarm at your home."

"It was me," Emma told him.

"I'll need your code word, Ms. McKinley."

"Harvard."

"Thank you, ma'am."

As she was replacing the receiver on the cradle, Jeanine and David came down the stairs. Jeanine was wearing a faded terrycloth robe and David was wearing basketball shorts and a T-shirt.

"What happened?" Jeanine asked. Then seeing Emma's hand, she added, "Are you hurt?"

Emma shook her head. "It's just paint," she said, having learned as much from the two previous encounters with the 'bloody' flower delivery guy. "Conner got the results on the other two today."

Going to the sink, she washed her hands and listened as her breathing returned to normal. Her rapid heartbeat was another matter. "I accidentally set off the alarm. Sorry; I didn't mean to wake you two."

Jeanine was looking at the flower. "What kind of person would do this to a chrysanthemum?"

"The same one who did it to a tulip and a lily on the porch for me to find," she answered.

"Always with the blood effect but the flower is different?" David asked.

Emma nodded. "But that's a dead end. I called a nursery and all these flowers are readily available this time of year. Sold in most grocery stores, in fact."

"Maybe you should call the sheriff," Jeanine suggested.

Emma shook her head. "I'll tell him tomorrow. I'm really sorry I disturbed everyone. Please go back to bed."

"Can I make you some tea?" Jeanine offered.

Emma smiled. "Thank you, but no. Please go back to sleep."

It took some insistence on her part, but Jeanine and David finally ended up returning to their rooms. Emma turned off the lights downstairs and followed them up five minutes later. Just because she could, she tried her sister's cell again. Again, it went to voicemail.

She glanced at her bedside clock: one a.m. She was far too keyed up to sleep so she got out of bed and returned to the kitchen. There, she made herself a mug of decaf coffee. Then she went to her office and opened the large file folder Conner had given her earlier in the evening.

Since he was presumably busy tracking down her sister's cell records, she might as well return the favor and read the life and times of his divorce and custody battle.

"Nice," she muttered as she read the initial pleadings. The former Mrs. Kavanaugh and her attorney had thrown every possible accusation his way, save for child abuse. They did allege abandonment since Conner's job took him away at any and all times of the day and night.

They glossed over the affair she'd been having with her boss and for some reason the presiding family court judge had sided with Conner's wife.

She sipped her fake coffee as she read through the custody saga. The ex had even filed to restrict visitation because Conner took Sam with him to the prison to visit her uncle the murderer. Through the attached affidavits Emma learned more about Michael Kavanaugh's crime and conviction, and his subsequent exemplary life inside prison.

Grabbing a legal pad, she made several notes as she went along. As far as she could tell, Conner had a pretty good case for material change in circumstances. He was now the sheriff, so he had more control over his schedule, and his right to see his daughter was severely restricted by his ex's move to Chicago. There was only one unknown in the equation. Samantha. Because she was sixteen, the judge would take her testimony in camera and her desires would be paramount to the outcome. If Samantha didn't want to spend more time with her father, then Conner would be screwed. However, from what Emma had seen Sam adored her father, and she didn't doubt for a second that the girl would be outspoken about that if and when asked.

Her cell chirped and she grabbed it in a nanosecond. "Amelia?"

"Sorry," Conner said. "Did I wake you?"

Dawn was just breaking on the horizon, spilling weak light into the room. "God, no. I was just finishing up your divorce file."

"I told you not to bother with that until we find Amelia."

"Did you get the subpoena for her cellphone?"

"Not yet. Apparently, I have to wait for someone from the cell carrier's legal compliance division to get into the office at eight this morning."

Emma rolled her eyes and sighed. "That's stupid."

"How are you holding up?"

"I'm doing a pretty good job at lying to myself. Ya know, concentrating on the fact that she went willingly."

"That's good."

"But in reality, she went willingly into a car with stolen plates, so that worries me. Oh," she began as she set aside her pen, "I had another special delivery tonight."

"What?"

"Another flower dipped in red paint."

Conner let out an expletive. "I don't suppose your video system covers the mailbox?"

"No. It's too far away from the cameras mounted on the house."

"Do you need me to come over?" he asked.

Yes. Selfish. But it would be wonderful to be cradled in his arms. It dawned on her that Conner made her feel safe. She had never had that feeling before and it was exhilarating and scary. "No, I'm fine," she fibbed.

"Well, I've been thinking."

"About?" she asked.

"Could this be a ransom situation?"

Emma ran her fingers through her hair. "No one has made contact."

"*Yet.* I have to ask. How well off are you?"

"I got a twenty-million-dollar settlement."

He whistled. "Who knows about that?"

"The case was settled and the records sealed."

"But you've been spending money in Purdue like you had a tree made out of it in your backyard. Maybe someone noticed."

"Maybe," she muttered as she pondered the thought. "But if that's the case, why haven't I been contacted?"

"I didn't say this was a job cooked up by a genius. Just throwing it out as a possibility."

"So, should I put up flyers or something?"

"Not yet," Conner cautioned. "You don't want to do anything to antagonize her captors. Assuming this is a kidnapping. Which seems to fit the evidence we have so far. It would explain the use of a lure and the precaution of changing out the license plate."

"I'll pay anything to get her back," Emma said.

"Purdue has its share of criminals, but I can't think of any-one around here smart enough to pull this off. So, could this be someone from your past? Maybe someone you repre-sented?"

"I doubt it," she answered. "I left New York quickly and quietly and no one can connect me to Purdue. Except…"

"Except?"

Emma hesitated. "Can we save this conversation for later this morning?"

"Time is a commodity here, Emma. If there's something I should know, tell me now."

"It's not something I want to do over the phone."

"Fine. I'll be there in thirty minutes."

As she put on a fresh pair of jeans and a boat neck tee, Emma tried to rehearse what she would say. In all the scenarios passing through her brain, they all ended with Conner storming out of her house. Sadness made her chest tight as she applied a small amount of makeup so she didn't look like death warmed over. Her final act was to make a pot of real coffee. Then she waited for what felt like an eternity but was actually a scant seven minutes.

She'd killed the alarm and opened the door before he fin-ished climbing the steps. She placed her finger to her lips. "David and Jeanine are sleeping."

Conner wasn't wearing his uniform. Instead he was dressed in jeans and a T-shirt. The pale blue shirt accented his eyes and clung to his muscled torso like a second skin.

His jeans hung low on his hips, inspiring all sorts of inappropriate thoughts on her part.

"Coffee?"

He nodded.

"Cream? Sugar?"

"Black is fine."

As she led him toward her office she felt nerves coil in her stomach. Emma had to keep reminding herself that telling Conner the truth could help find Amelia, and that had to be her first priority. Still, telling the man she'd been dishonest from day one wasn't something she was relishing.

She pointed him toward the empty chair across from her desk. As a stalling tactic, she went over her conclusions about his custody issues. "So, you're going to have to get Sam's feelings on all this or it won't be worth the effort of filing. The judge will place great weight on what she wants."

"Thanks," he said.

"You have a good case," she told him. "I'd be happy to draw up the petition if you'd like."

His smile reached his eyes. "Thanks for that. But let's focus on your sister."

Emma inhaled deeply and let her breath out slowly. Her eyes scanned his face, and she catalogued everything she liked about him just in case he stormed out the door.

"Well?" he prompted.

Emma placed her hands on the desk and made a small circle with her index finger. "I didn't come to Purdue by accident."

"I already know that Elgin found out about you from one of your law professors."

Emma shook her head. "I keep forgetting about the Purdue gossip channel."

She squeezed her eyes shut for a second, then blurted out, "I'm not Emma McKinley."

"What?"

"Technically I am." She nervously reached up and began twisting a lock of hair around her finger. "My name was changed when I was eleven. I was born Emily Stevens."

"Were you adopted?"

She shook her head. "Emily Hodges as in daughter of Courtland Hodges."

She watched as recognition dawned.

"The assassin?"

"Yes."

He leaned back in his chair. "Why would you want to come to Purdue after what your father did here twenty years ago?"

She opened her desk drawer and took out the envelope of clippings and passed them across the desk. "Someone has been sending these to me for six months. At first I ignored them because it was a closed chapter in my life."

"But now you're not so sure he really was the killer?"

She shrugged. "Someone wanted me to come here and look into the case. I wasn't interested until my mother became ill and I found this in her dresser." Emma reached in and took out the time-share promotional brochure. It was tri-fold, with a picture on the back she ignored as she folded it so Conner to see the wording of the invite. "I never knew why my father did what he did but I think maybe it has something to do with this time-share thing."

"You think he killed a sitting president over a vacation rental?" Conner asked with a definite edge in his voice.

"I don't know why he did it and thanks to Kenny Simms, no one will ever know. Maybe if he wouldn't have shot my father on the scene, we would know my father's motivation."

"So, you aren't here to prove there was some Oswaldlike conspiracy at play?"

Emma's whole body suddenly felt tight. "I came to grips with what my father did years ago."

"Then why the name change?" he asked.

"My mother was being haunted by the press and by the various governmental commissions examining the assassination. To protect my sister and me, she changed our names and moved us from Washington, D.C., to north Georgia. She gave us the gift of a relatively normal childhood."

"What about the lawsuit?"

"I worked for a very prestigious law firm in New York and I stupidly confided in a guy I thought was my friend. He told the partners and they fired me. I sued them for wrongful termination and won."

"Is that why you didn't tell me?" he asked.

She nodded. "I swore after the New York fiasco I'd never tell another soul. Hell, Amelia is engaged and she hasn't even told her fiancé yet."

Conner stood, stuffing the clippings into the envelope as he did. "Can I keep these?"

"For what?"

"I want to run them for prints. Maybe find out who lured you here in the first place."

Emma blinked. "You're not pissed at me for not telling you about my past?"

"Nope. I'm definitely pissed. But I'll get over it."

CHAPTER SEVENTEEN

Emma called in to work and said she'd be in late if at all, just in case Conner was right and this was some whack job of a kidnapping. Not an ideal way to make an impression on her new boss; it did seem, however, to be her best option.

"Did you sleep at all?" Jeanine asked when she came down wearing a faded floral dress and a well-worn sweater.

Emma just shrugged. "You might want to make a fresh pot of coffee or use the Keurig. The stuff I made is really bitter."

"I'll take care of it," she said, though she remained lingering in the doorway of Emma's office.

"Yes?" Emma prompted.

"I need to tell you something."

"Go ahead."

"I caught Jess and Sam in here last night when you were out with the sheriff." She was wringing her hands. "I was gonna to tell you when you got home but then…"

"Do you know what they were doing in here?" she asked.

Jeanine frowned. "Nothing good," she insisted. "I reminded them both that this was your private space and I ordered them into the living room."

"May I talk to David when he gets up?"

"Feel free," Jeanine said. "And if you want us to leave because—"

"I don't want you to leave. I just want to reinforce the rules with him. And with Sam."

Jeanine checked her watch. "It'll be a little while before Sam gets here. Do you want to talk to them together or separately?"

"Separately," Emma decided.

"I'll get David," she said before spinning on the ball of her foot and leaving the office.

Emma would be lying if she said she wasn't disappointed. She'd had such hope for David, and it definitely did not bode well that he'd broken one of her cardinal rules in the first weeks.

Emma was absently twisting her hair into a ponytail when a very disheveled-looking David was escorted down the stairs and virtually shoved into the room by his mother. He was still half-asleep but since he wouldn't make direct eye contact, she figured he knew exactly why he'd been summoned.

He rubbed his face, then said, "I can explain."

"I'm ready to listen," Emma said as she sat back in her chair and crossed her arms.

"Your computer has a bigger and better processor than mine."

"And?"

"I heard you talking to the sheriff about your sister's cell phone records and I thought maybe I could save you some time and just hack into her account."

Emma uncrossed her arms. "You can do that?"

He nodded. "Maybe. I overheard her number and the carrier. Mom just found us in here before I had a chance to try."

Emma relinquished her seat. "Let's see what you can do," she said, motioning David around the desk.

David's fingers flew across the keyboard. The screen went from normal to dark and suddenly a bunch of numbers and symbols scrolled quickly down the screen. "Are you sure you know what you're doing?" she asked.

"One sec," he said. "Okay, I'm in."

Emma found herself staring at the cell provider's home screen. "Now what?"

"Do you happen to know her password?"

Emma shook her head.

"That will be a problem." David frowned. "This is a three strikes system."

"In English?"

"If you enter an incorrect password more than three times you're automatically locked out of the system."

"That sucks."

"Ideas?"

Emma began to pace her office. She tried to think of

all the things that her sister might have used. Amelia had changed carriers three months ago, just after her engagement to Brody. She gave David the date of Brody's proposal but that didn't work.

Strike one.

She glanced at the clock, then reached for the phone.

"Hello?" came a gravelly male voice on the other end.

Emma winced. It was barely seven o'clock. "Brody, it's Em. Did I wake you?"

She heard him clear his throat. "My alarm was about to go off anyway. Reggie called me last night. She said Amelia had taken a side trip from Purdue?"

"Actually," she said gently, "she's sort of disappeared."

Brody wigged out for a few minutes before she could get him back under control. "Do you know the password for her cell account?"

"Her Facebook password is Twins1986. Maybe she uses that for everything."

Emma repeated the potential password to David.

Strike Two.

She thanked Brody and promised to keep him abreast of things in Purdue but declined his offer to come down. Amelia would be furious if Emma did anything to alert Brody to their past. Besides, Emma didn't want or need him underfoot.

The doorbell chimed, bringing Emma back to the present. She stepped into the hallway to find Willis Maddox standing in her foyer. "Good morning, ma'am," he greeted.

"What can I do for you?"

"I need to buy some sod for the backyard and I was wondering if I could rent a truck for a few hours so I can do it all in one trip. It's only nineteen-ninety-nine for the rental."

"Of course," Emma said. She went to her purse and took forty dollars out of her wallet. She handed him the money and Willis stared at it for a second.

"This is too much," he said, trying to hand her back one of the twenties.

"There might be tax," she explained. "Oh, and I called the home improvement place and we've got an account there now, so just tell them to bill the sod to my account. Wait. Do you have a driver's license?"

"Good for one more year," he said with pride. "I had to take the test four times but I finally got it."

Emma smiled. "Okay, then. Thank you."

Willis left the house and Emma went back to David, who asked her, "What about her social security number or her birthday?"

Exhaling slowly, she ask, "What's the most common password?"

"'Password.'"

"Seriously?" she asked.

David nodded. "Want me to try that?"

Emma hesitated, then said, "Why not."

She watched as he typed in the word, then paused before hitting the enter key.

Strike three.

Damn.

"How long will we be locked out of the account?" she asked.

"Usually it's a twenty-four-hour hold, but I might be able to get around that. Want me to keep trying?"

Emma nodded, then went to refill her coffee. In the kitchen she found Jeanine making a huge breakfast of eggs, hash brown potatoes, and bacon. Jeanine was working the stove like a short order cook, quick and proficient.

Emma snagged a strip of bacon. "How do you manage to get everything to the table hot at the same time?"

"Practice," she answered. She stopped, spatula in hand, and met Emma's gaze. "Are you going to fire me?" she asked.

"God, no," Emma answered immediately. "I mean, I'm not thrilled that David and Samantha were in my office, but he only did that to try and help."

Jeanine seemed to relax instantly. "I was up worried all night, afraid that you'd toss me out on my ear and I'd end up back with Skeeter."

"Not going to happen," Emma promised. "I'm not Renae Burke."

Jeanine scoffed. "You don't have to tell me. That woman is a whole different kinda animal."

"How so?" Emma asked as she refilled her coffee mug, then leaned with her back against the counter. She was careful to control her tone as to not sound overly curious and make Jeanine suspicious.

"For a well-bred woman, she sure is rude. I'll never understand how Mary has worked for her for so long." Jeanine started to scramble eggs. "She's demanding and secretive."

Again, Emma tried not to sound too eager, but again she asked, "How so?"

"Well," Jeanine said on a breath. "Silly stuff. I had to fold the laundry but I wasn't allowed to put it in the dresser. Just on the edge of the bed. Like I was going to trifle through her belongings."

"That's a little strange."

"Then there were the times when she'd practically banish me."

"What?"

Jeanine just shrugged. "Sometimes she would get a call, then the next thing I know she'd send me home for the day."

"Do you know why?"

"Well, one day, I was in the middle of buffing the dining room floor and she came in and told me to leave, but I had to explain I had to get the wax up off the floor before it dried and screwed up the wood. She wasn't happy and when the doorbell rang, she raced to answer it and then took whoever came over right on back into her study and closed the door."

"Do you know who it was?"

"Never saw him before or since."

"Maybe it was just a business deal," Emma suggested.

Jeanine shook her head. "Mrs. Burke acted like I was invisible when she discussed business with people. That was the only time I can ever remember her even answering her own front door."

"How long ago was this?"

"Maybe six months," Jeanine said as she took the pan

off the stove and transferred the eggs to a platter. "Let's get some food in you," she said. "You didn't eat last night and you need to keep your strength up."

Maybe she was too worried about Amelia, or perhaps she'd had too much coffee. At any rate, Emma barely touched the mountain of food Jeanine prepared. She was carrying her plate to the sink when the doorbell rang.

Conner, decked out in his uniform, had Samantha in tow. He was also holding an intriguing manila envelope.

"Good morning," she greeted him as he moved past her. She caught the faint, woodsy scent of his cologne and it had an instant, calming effect on her.

Based on the look on Samantha's face, David must have given Conner's daughter a heads up on the office violation situation.

"I got the phone records," Conner said as he handed over the envelope.

Emma slipped her fingernail beneath the flap and tore. Inside were three pages of records. She immediately flipped to the previous day and scanned the phone numbers. "This one is the hospital my mom's in. This one is her friend Regina's number. What are these two?" she asked, pointing to one entry between the call to the hospital and another entry a few minutes after her call to Regina.

Conner came and looked over her shoulder. He was close enough so she could feel the heat coming off his body. His warm breath fell on her neck. The combination made it hard for her to concentrate on the phone records because she was remembering—vividly—what it was like to be in his arms, being kissed senseless. When he stepped back, she felt abandoned and sad.

"I asked our tech guy and he said those calls were most likely from a burner phone."

"Great," Emma groused. "They can't be traced."

"But they can be triangulated," he explained. "I've got our tech division working with the phone company right now so we can see where your sister's phone has been pinging since she got into that Crown Vic."

Her hopes soared. "That's great."

Conner's expression grew more serious. "I have more news."

"What?" Emma asked, heart dropping at his grim expression.

"I had our lab run the prints off those news clippings."

"And?"

"Yours, which are on file from when you were admitted to the state bar association."

"To be expected."

Conner looked past Emma to David, who was standing in the hallway next to Samantha. "David Segan's prints were on them."

Emma turned and gave him a withering look. "I thought you only went into my office to use my computer."

"I may have looked around a little," he admitted with his head hung low.

"Two sets of unidentifiable prints."

"So, whoever was sending the clippings to me isn't in the system."

"You didn't let me finish."

"Sorry."

"There was one other set of prints."

"Belonging to…?"

"Your boss, Elgin Hale."

CHAPTER EIGHTEEN

Emma was stunned. Elgin? Seriously?

"I don't understand," she mumbled as she tried to digest this unforeseen complication. What could Elgin hope to gain by luring her to Purdue? "I don't remember him being in any of the news clippings I read about. Was he even at the assassination?"

"He was a public defender back then," Conner said. "I checked."

His radio crackled to life. "Go ahead for Kavanaugh," he said into the receiver.

"We've got a location on that cell number."

Emma's heart stopped.

"Give it to me."

"One-hundred yards east of the logging road off highway fifty-two."

"I'm heading there now. Have Hammond and Miller meet me there. Everybody goes in quiet. Got it?"

"Yes sir."

Emma grabbed her purse and her gun from the drawer in the foyer table.

"What do you think you're doing?" Conner asked as he clipped the radio back to his shoulder.

"I'm coming with you," she stated, practically daring him to contradict her. "Amelia could be hurt or frightened."

Conner pointed to her gun. "So you're going to shoot her?"

"It's just a precaution. We don't know what will happen when we get there." She stuffed the gun in her bag and headed for the door. "Coming?" she asked.

"This is a bad idea," he mumbled as he followed her out to his SUV.

Once they were belted in and on their way, he said, "Under no circumstances are you to get out of this car. Understood?"

"But—"

"No buts. I should not have agreed to let you come along."

"Amelia is my sister," Emma said softly.

"I know that. But my feelings for you clouded my decision making and I don't like that."

Emma stilled in her seat. "I thought you were pissed at me."

"I am," he admitted easily. "You should have told me the truth before we slept together."

"As I remember it, we didn't do a lot of talking that night."

"You had the entire time we were having dinner," he reminded her with a quick glance in her direction.

"Right. 'My father killed a sitting president' is usually my first-date choice of conversations." Emma adjusted her seatbelt. "Can't you drive any faster?"

"We're going ninety-five."

She was suddenly gripped with a sense of dread. "The phone triangulation doesn't mean she's alive, does it."

Conner reached over and squeezed her thigh through her jeans. "You can't think like that."

Reflexively, she covered his hand with hers and drew comfort from the contact. She glanced out the window, running possible scenarios through her head. None of them were good. She tried to concentrate on the area, but there wasn't much to see except an old growth pine forest and the occasional fan palm. They were on a two-lane road that made the tires go *thump-thump* every quarter mile or so.

"The turnoff is up ahead," Conner said as he killed the lights atop the SUV. "I'll say it again: you stay in the car."

Conner went in about fifty yards, then parked the car diagonally, partially blocking the logging road.

As he got out of the car, he drew his weapon and cautiously began moving down the road.

Emma's heart was racing, which got even worse when Conner was out of sight. She kept glancing at both sides of the road, wondering when the other deputies would show up so Conner wouldn't be on his own. Hell, there could be more than one kidnapper.

With no backup in sight and her heart pounding in her

ears, Emma retrieved her gun and stepped out of the vehicle. Pine straw crunched beneath her feet and she listened above the din of insects for any other sound. It was warming up and she was so nervous that she began to perspire.

"Stop!" she heard Conner call.

She quickened her pace but only for a second, when she heard the crackle of gunfire. Emma hugged the tree line as she moved toward the sound. She had gone about twenty yards when she spotted Conner crouched behind a fallen tree trunk. He had his gun trained on an old, abandoned-looking mobile home.

She worked her way toward him.

"You were supposed to stay in the car," he said when she fell into place beside him.

"I heard shots."

Emma looked around and found the landscape odd. She was kneeling on pavers covered by years of debris. The trailer was dilapidated but she could just make out a short walkway still visible beneath the overgrowth. "What is this place?" she whispered.

"It was supposed to be a development project years ago but it fell through."

"Who owns it?"

"How should I know?" Conner answered. "I'm working here."

"Any sighting of Amelia?"

"Yes."

Relief flooded her body. "That's—"

There was a barrage of gunfire and Emma found herself

tossed down, face first into the pine straw. She felt Conner's weight on top of her as the gunfire continued unabated.

After what felt like an eternity, Conner rolled off her at the sound of an engine revving.

Emma struggled to her feet just as the taillights of a Crown Vic disappeared down the unpaved road. Conner shot at the tires but missed.

Now she had her sights set on the trailer. Emma went around the tree she'd used for cover and began running toward the doorway. Her body was tense and she was keenly aware of everything around her—sights, sounds, smells—anything that might present a problem. But there was nothing but the natural sounds of the swampy land.

The door was off the hinges, and she reached out and shoved it aside. "Amelia!"

"Mmmmmmmmmm!"

Following the sound, Emma found her sister in a back room that had been set up as an office. She was tied to a plastic chair and had duct tape over her mouth and around her wrists. Tears streamed down her dirty cheeks. Emma gave her a hug and whispered, "It's all over now."

"Back off," Conner said as he entered the cabin.

Emma turned and met his gaze. "What are you talking about?"

"Don't touch anything." Then he turned his attention to Amelia. "I know this is horrible but I need you to hang on for just a minute while I get some evidence collection bags. There could be DNA or fingerprints on that duct tape and we'll need that when we bring your kidnapper to trial."

Amelia hesitated for a few seconds, then nodded.

"Stay with her," he told Emma. "I'll be back in a few minutes. I've got to call for an ambulance."

It was only after he'd said that that Emma really looked at her sister. There was dried blood in her hair, and large bruises on her calves seemed to indicate she'd been hit with some sort of pole-like object more than once. Her bare feet were also bloodied. Emma felt instantly sick to her stomach. Amelia had been tortured, but why?

She had to wait nearly five minutes to begin peppering her sister with questions. Conner carefully sliced away the duct tape and placed it in clear evidence bags.

"Are you okay?" Emma asked.

"No," Amelia answered on a gulp of air. "They hit me with a tire iron. My head, my legs and the soles of my feet."

Emma asked, "Do you know why?"

Amelia met her gaze. "You."

"Me?"

"I got a call at the airport telling me you'd been taken and that I could save you if I followed the instructions of a man in a black Crown Victoria."

"You didn't think to call me to check out the story?"

"I was worried," Amelia insisted. "I thought maybe he knew that…" Her words trailed off as she looked over at Conner.

"He knows," Emma said. "I told him."

Amelia's eyes grew wide.

"Don't worry. He won't tell anyone."

"Brody?" Amelia asked about her fiancé.

"I played it low key. He's worried, but I didn't tell him you were actually kidnapped."

"How am I going to explain this to him?"

Conner half-coughed. "The truth will work."

"You don't know his family. They're very conservative."

"So what. We didn't do anything wrong," Emma argued.

"Um," Conner began. "Can you walk me through what happened?"

"I was at the airport and I got a call. The caller said he had Emma and if I ever wanted to see her again, I'd meet a man driving a black Crown Victoria who'd be pulling up any second."

"You should have called me before you got into that car," Emma said.

"I was panicked," Amelia returned tersely. "So, I get in and he drives off and brings me here."

"Describe him," Conner said.

Amelia shook her head. "I can only tell you he was about six feet tall. Maybe one hundred eighty pounds. Very muscular."

"What did he look like?" Emma pressed.

"He always had on a ski mask," Amelia explained. "All I know is he had blue eyes."

"Could you recognize the eyes again?"

Amelia shrugged. "Maybe. But I'd know his voice anywhere. He kept asking me the same stuff over and over."

"What stuff?" Emma asked.

"Mostly about you. How much you knew about the assassination. Why you were in Purdue. If anyone was helping you. That sort of stuff. I tried to tell him you were genuinely working for the Public Defender and that we had come to terms with our dad being a killer years ago."

"But he didn't buy it?"

She shook her head and Emma watched as she visibly shivered. "He was one sadistic bastard. He really seemed to like punishing me. Even after the other guy told him to lay off."

"'Other guy?'" Emma and Conner said in unison.

"Someone was here last night. They spoke outside the trailer, so I had to strain to listen."

"Did he say anything else?"

"Not that I could make out."

The sound of approaching sirens cut through the serenity of the location. "I'm going to send a deputy to the hospital with you," Conner said.

Amelia turned to Emma. "Will you be with me?"

Emma shook her head. "I have an errand to run and then I'll be there."

"What kind of errand is more important than me?" Amelia asked.

"I have to go talk to my boss," she answered.

"Not alone," Conner warned.

"Elgin doesn't fit the physical description of her kidnapper."

"But he could have been the second guy."

"I don't think so."

"He's the only other person in Purdue who knows who you really are."

"Point."

The paramedics came in then and began transferring a battered and bruised Amelia to a stretcher. Seeing her sister like that shook her to the core. And it made little sense. Even if someone knew that Emma and Amelia were the daughters of the assassin, Emma couldn't understand why that information would inspire this sort of reaction or violence. What had pushed the kidnapper over the edge? Or even warranted kidnapping in the first place? She was missing something.

Something important.

CHAPTER NINETEEN

This is something I have to do alone," Emma insisted when he drove her back to her house to pick up her car.

Conner blocked her with his body. "Not smart. You don't know how involved Elgin is in all of this. Let me come with you."

She felt the heat emanating off his body and inhaled the clean, woodsy scent of soap on his skin. How tempting to know that all she had to do was reach out and pull him to her. Great minds—because the next thing she knew, she was in his arms and his mouth claimed hers.

His large hands ran up and down her body, every so often just brushing the sides of her breasts. Weak in the knees, head swimming, Emma sank into the kiss. It felt so good, so right to be wrapped in his embrace. The kiss was incredible, too. He nibbled her lower lip, then ran his tongue against the sensitive place on her mouth. Pressed against him, she felt the power of his arousal against her belly. All she had to do was lead him the few feet into her bedroom and let everything else happen naturally.

She started to do that, but met resistance. Conner reached up, ended the kiss and cradled her face between his palms. She looked into his blue eyes and saw raw passion, which further confused her.

"What?"

"Your sister's in the hospital. Your mother's in poor health and at least two people are trying to run you out of town. The last thing you need is another complication."

"Having sex with you is not a complication," Emma said seductively.

Conner released her to step back. "It is for me. I don't want to be just a distraction while things in your life are in turmoil."

"What *do* you want?"

"I'm not sure yet." He gave her a steady look and tucked his fingers into the front pockets of his jeans. "I just know that until we figure out why you've been receiving threats and your sister was kidnapped and tortured, the sex stops. And don't think for a minute this is easy for me. I want you, Emma. You know that."

A shiver of desire ran down her spine. "I want you, too."

"Well, we'll just have to deal with that later."

"Right. Now I go see Elgin."

"No. *We* go see Elgin. Until we can rule him out as Bad Guy Number Two, you're not going anywhere without me glued to your side."

Emma rolled her eyes. "I'm going to the office. Do you

really think there's anything he can do to me in a public place?"

He stubbornly stood his ground. "I'm not willing to take that chance."

"Fine," she sighed. Conner shifted to let her pass.

It didn't take them long to reach her building. With Conner on her heels, she walked directly to Elgin's office. He looked up at her with surprise. "Emma? I thought you were taking the day."

"I was," she said, standing behind one of the visitor chairs. Conner closed the office door, then stood beside her.

"Sheriff," Elgin acknowledged.

"I know you were the one who sent me the news clippings. I want to know why," Emma said without preamble.

Elgin's neck reddened above his shirt collar. "I don't know—"

"Don't even try that," Emma insisted. "Your prints are all over them."

Elgin leaned back in his chair and steepled his fingertips. After a long pause he said, "Okay. It was me."

"Why?"

"When the president was assassinated I was a new public defender. I thought then, and I think now, that there are too many unanswered questions. I just thought if you got curious…"

"Curious about what?" Emma frowned and dug her fingers into the chair back. Elgin's response wasn't what she'd expected at all. She wanted answers and now she had more damned questions. "My father was killed on the scene and the rifle recovered next to his body was the murder weapon."

"But why?" Elgin pressed. "Why did your father fly from D.C. to Florida to kill a president, when it was later discovered that your father had no interest in politics and didn't even vote?"

"That wasn't in any clipping," Emma stated.

"Your mother told me," Elgin said.

Emma blinked. "My mother?"

"I tracked her down a few years back and after some begging and groveling on my part, she agreed to talk to me."

"My mother accepts the historical accuracy of the events."

"Not completely," Elgin countered. "Like me, she couldn't understand the why of it."

"So once my mother got sick you decided to track me down and lure me to Purdue?"

He shrugged. "I thought being here might inspire your interest."

"So far it's just nearly gotten my sister killed, and I've been shot at, and had bloody-looking flowers delivered to my house three times. Who else knows who I am?"

Elgin fervently shook his head. "No one. I haven't told a soul."

"At least two other people know," Emma said, then she recounted her sister's kidnapping and torture. "So, whatever you've put into place has backfired bigtime."

"I never meant for you or your sister to come to any harm. And I never thought anyone would put the pieces together."

"How did you?" Emma asked.

"A Lexus-Nexus search on your names. I found the court filings for change of name and then it was just a matter of searching DMV records. The fact that you had Larry Grisom as a law professor was pure coincidence. When I called him about you he assumed it was to offer you a job. That's the truth."

"Why didn't you just tell me all this from the start?" Emma asked.

"That whole debacle in New York," Elgin replied. "I figured that situation might have left a bad taste in your mouth about the assassination, so I thought better of it."

"I know this town. Everyone here knew about the flowers and the fact that someone took a shot at my house. But when weird things started happening," Emma prompted. "You didn't think to give me a heads up?"

"You didn't think they were *things*," he said. "I was taking my cue from you."

Conner took a seat, indicating for Emma to do the same. "So what do they gain by kidnapping Amelia?"

"'They'?" Elgin asked.

"My sister said a second man came in the night," Emma replied.

Elgin's face grew animated. "That means there *is* a conspiracy."

"A conspiracy to do *what*?" Conner asked.

"To run Emma and Amelia out of town, I guess. At any rate, it tends to prove my theory that more was going on the night of the assassination than just the act of a lone, crazed gunman."

Emma folded her hands and rested them on the seatback. She kept her head down as she said, "But he was there and he was shot and the gun that killed the president and the governor was right next to him. I've seen the evidence photos."

"You have?" Conner asked.

She nodded. "They've been on television."

"That's cold," Conner muttered.

Emma turned her attention to Elgin. "Are you sure you haven't told anyone about me?"

* * *

"It's dusty in here," Emma groused as she used her shirt sleeve to wipe the dust off another box. *Wrong year.* "And I have to have tea with Renae Burke in a little while."

"You don't have to be here," Conner said. "In fact, I'm not sure what's in the file on the assassination, so it's probably best that you not look at it until after I've had a chance to go through it."

"You obviously don't get the History channel," she returned. "They do a retrospective almost every year. One year they used gel dummies with pig flesh to prove my father was the only possible killer since he was the only person in the balcony of the theater."

"That's disgusting."

"I thought about writing them a strongly worded letter the first time I saw it, but I was only sixteen and I figured they'd think I was biased."

Conner stopped walking down the row of the evidence

warehouse they were in and pulled her against him. It was nice to smell his cologne instead of the musty, dank scent of moldy paper. The rows were lit by bare lights hanging from the ceiling, swaying softly on the breeze made by large fans mounted along the walls.

"Maybe you should go to the hospital to be with your sister," he said as he placed a soft kiss against her brow.

"I've already talked to her twice. They're keeping her overnight because she's dehydrated. I promised to stop by later. Amelia told me she doesn't need me there to watch her IV drip."

He rubbed his hand up and down her back, sending little shivers through her system. "Maybe she needs moral support. Besides, I can go through the file without you."

"No way," Emma said emphatically.

"Well, at least let me edit it. There's probably some stuff in there you won't want to see."

"Fair enough," she relented, but she didn't step out of his embrace. Instead she got up on tiptoes and tried to kiss him.

Conner gently set her away from him.

She was still looking in his eyes. "Still pissed?"

"Almost over it," he said. "I understand why you guarded your privacy."

"Thank you."

"But I don't think that's the kind of thing you should hide from the guy you're sleeping with."

"That makes me sound like the town slut," she said with annoyance. "For whatever reason, things between us moved fast but that doesn't make me—"

"I never said it did. Don't take it that way." Conner moved farther down the corridor. "Jackpot."

* * *

Emma sneezed four times as she carried two of the five boxes from the evidence storage unit to Conner's car. It felt good to get out of that building and back into the sunshine. She and Conner piled the boxes into the back of the SUV and drove them to the sheriff's office.

They carried everything into a large conference room. Emma was keenly aware of people staring. "What is that about?" she asked Conner.

"Probably J.T.," he said.

"J.T.?" she repeated.

"He was the paramedic who responded to the scene this morning. He's a good friend of Sally's. Sally works the lunch shift at Stella's, so…"

"Everyone in town knows about Amelia and me?"

Conner shook his head. "Probably they just know that your sister was tortured. That's news enough. Unless you think Amelia would tell a total stranger why she'd been taken hostage?"

"God no," Emma insisted. "She'd rather gnaw off her own tongue. I hate being stared at."

"Then you chose an interesting line of work."

"You think the courtroom is a theater?"

"I think sometimes the most articulate attorney wins. That isn't always justice."

She glanced at him and discovered his features were taut and fixed. "Does that have anything to do with your brother being in prison?"

Conner nodded. "And Hayden Blackwell keeping him there all these years. He promised to show up at every parole hearing and makes it sound as if Michael went on a major shooting rampage that night instead of what really happened."

"When is his parole hearing?"

"Three weeks. My brothers and I will all be there. Hopefully that will help."

"I'm sure it will. Are your brothers all upstanding members of the community?"

Conner nodded. "Declan is a private detective and Jack is like you. He's an attorney."

"Criminal defense?"

"Yeah. Pretty much anything. He just got married a few months ago, and they have a little girl named Mia."

"Is Declan married?"

Conner half-snorted, half-grunted. "I don't think there's a woman on the planet who would want to take him on."

"Why?"

"He always has to be right. Even when he's wrong. Everything has to be done his way."

Emma whistled. "I know the type."

Conner lifted the corner of one box and asked, "Are you sure you're up to this?"

"Oh, yeah," she said as she opened her box.

Carefully, she laid the evidence out on the table in

groups—physical evidence, written reports, expert consultations. She wasn't sure what to do with the videotape she found so she placed it in its own pile.

Conner did the same. Which worked out well until he opened the box with all the photographs, some of which were very graphic. "I'll save these for later," he said, gathering up the pictures of her dead father.

"It's okay," she insisted, touching his sleeve. Her eyes were immediately drawn to a photograph of the president and the governor taken just after the gunshots had sounded. The president was on the ground and Rossner was half on top of him. "What did witnesses say about the shots?" she asked as she went back to the pile of witness statements. She randomly checked about twenty of them. "They all claim three shots were fired."

"One hit the president and one hit the governor," Conner confirmed. "The first one hit the president. The second one hit the governor's campaign manager—Renae Burke's husband—and the final shot killed Governor Rossner."

"That doesn't make sense," Emma argued.

"What doesn't?"

"If the president was the target, then why fire the two additional shots?" she mused aloud. "Unless the president wasn't the primary target."

CHAPTER TWENTY

Find any ballistics reports?" Conner asked. "This is just the local stuff, remember. The official reports are in Washington with the Department of Justice."

Emma rifled through three boxes before she found a schematic of the shooting. Attached to the crude drawing was a report. "They did a triangulation but it doesn't match the drawing," she said. "See"—she placed both pages on the table in front of him—"based on the shells recovered, this shows a shooter moving left to right, but if you look at the witness statements, the people were shot in a right-to-left pattern."

"So the local ballistics guys got it wrong?" Conner asked.

She looked at the report. "Do any of these people still work here?" she asked.

Conner shook his head. "No. One's dead and the other one is retired."

"Do you think he'd talk to us?"

"I'll call him and set it up." Conner glanced at his watch. "Shouldn't you be going home to gussy up for your tea with Renae Burke?"

Emma rolled her eyes. "I'd love to cancel."

"Remember, she was there that night. Maybe you can get her to open up."

"Which is the only reason I'm going," Emma told him. "Call me on my cell if you find anything else interesting."

"I will."

* * *

Emma raced home and was right on schedule until she stopped to collect the mail. Once again, and for the second time this week, she found a flower—this time a camellia—dipped in blood or paint or *whatever*, tucked in with her mail. As expected, neither Janine, David, nor Sam had noticed anything suspicious.

She tossed the flower in the garbage and allowed fear to follow her to her bedroom. The bloody flowers weren't part of a prank. Neither were the gunshots into her den. No, she'd been kidding herself. Someone knew who she was and obviously realized she was there to look into the assassination.

The irony was that she probably would have taken only a cursory glance at the records if it hadn't been for the flowers, the gunshots, and Amelia's kidnapping.

Sam and David were in the living room, working on his laptop. Jeanine was wherever the strong scent of pine was coming from. Emma went into her room, showered, and changed into a pale green shift dress and some strappy sandals. She added a long strand of pearls and carried a white sweater just in case it got cooler as the sun set. She made a quick call to the hospital before placing her gun and phone in her purse. She wasn't about to go flitting around without some protection.

As Emma was about to leave, David and Sam met her in the foyer.

"We know what the flowers mean!" Sam exclaimed.

David angled his laptop so she could see the screen. "Look here," he said. "Tulips, chrysanthemums, lilies, and camellias all meant death in Victorian England."

Immediately Emma thought of Renae Burke's Victorian mansion. Was it possible that the Queen of Purdue was the one behind the flower deliveries? No, Emma couldn't imagine that woman doing her own dirty work and besides, Amelia had been emphatic that two men had been involved in her kidnapping.

On her trip to Renae's she called Conner and told him about the meaning of the flowers.

"Turn the car around," he said curtly.

"Don't be silly," Emma said. "I've interviewed and represented serial killers. I can handle a society maven."

"But she's the only real link you've found besides Elgin."

"Which is why I called you. I wanted someone to know where I was, just in case."

"I don't have a good feeling about this," Conner warned.

"I'm not exactly looking forward to it," Emma admitted.

"Did you have any luck with the ballistics expert?"

"He gaffed me off," Conner said. "So I sent the stuff to the Florida Department of Law Enforcement's ballistics lab. I should get a response in about a week."

"A week? Seriously?"

"A twenty-year-old solved case isn't a high priority for them."

"What about a private expert?" Emma suggested. "I know a guy in New York who will probably do it overnight if we send him the information." Emma ticked off the address by rote. "I'll call him and give him a heads up."

"I'll make the necessary copies and FedEx them ASAP. Call me when you leave Renae's house."

"Why?" she asked with a smile. "Worried about me?"

"Always."

"But you're still pissed?"

There was a brief pause. "No, I'm over it now."

"Really? I'm forgiven?"

"Oh, you're more than forgiven."

Emma felt her heartbeat quicken. "What does that mean?"

"I'll tell you when I see you."

With that, he disconnected, leaving Emma feeling better than she'd felt in days. Yes, she was curious about what he might say, but she was more relieved than anything. She understood that because of the infidelity in his marriage Conner wasn't going to trust easily, but if he truly had forgiven her for keeping her identity a secret, then she was halfway home.

"And exactly what is *home*?" she mused aloud as she drove

along the two-lane road. The answer came to her in a flash. It was wherever Conner Kavanaugh was.

Admitting that to herself was exciting and scary. She'd had lovers before but none she would have considered commitment material. There was something different about Conner. Something about the way he made her feel. And that something, she acknowledged with happy resignation, was love. There; she'd said it. At least she'd said it in her brain. Now how could she say it out loud to Conner?

All thoughts of happily ever after went down the drain as she reached the massive iron gates that guarded the Burkes' property. Emma buzzed the callbox and announced herself. She glanced at her watch. She was only ten minutes late. Not good, but not a crime either.

She pulled into the horseshoe-shaped driveway and stopped near the front staircase. Instantly she noticed two things—first, there were flowerbeds everywhere and she recognized the at least one of the varieties left on her porch. Second, she noticed an attached six-car garage farther down the arched drive. She wondered if there might be a black Crown Victoria secreted in one of the stalls.

Emma checked her lipstick in the rearview mirror, opened her purse and slipped her phone inside, and then brushed her fingertips over her gun. There was something calming about the feel of cold steel beneath her fingertips.

She felt Renae Burke's green gaze on her before she reached the door. Though the older woman wore a smile, it didn't reach her eyes. "Why Emma, I'm so glad you made it. I was worried when I heard about your sister. How is the poor dear?"

"She's fine," Emma said as she stepped inside.

The house smelled of lemony baked goods with a slight undertone of cigar smoke. "Will the mayor be joining us?" she asked.

Renae waved a dismissive hand as she led Emma through to the parlor. "Maddison is off fundraising in Tallahassee today."

"He's running for the Senate?"

"Has his heart set on national office," Renae said with an exaggerated sigh. She had on a pair of white slacks paired with a simple beige cashmere sweater, and a gold necklace with a side broach of clustered emeralds and sapphires at her neckline. Matching emerald and sapphire earrings dangled from her earlobes. As usual, her hair was in an updo and her makeup was flawless.

And as usual, she left a vapor trail of perfume that Emma could taste as she took the chair Renae offered at the exquisitely set table. Renae picked up a little silver bell and jingled it.

Mary, the maid Jeanine had told Emma about, was dressed in a traditional black and white uniform, and arrived with a large tray. She transferred a platter and finger sandwich tower to the table along with two small pots and a selection of teas.

Emma's attention went to a watercolor hanging on the far wall. She remembered seeing it the last time she was at the house but this time she placed it instantly. It was the same image that was on the back of the time-share invitation that had drawn her father to Purdue twenty years earlier.

Without concern for Renae or the retreating Mary, Emma stood and walked over to the painting. "This is lovely," she said, then turned back to Renae.

"It's Pine Landing," Renae said. "It's a beautiful resort about seven miles from here."

"With Victorian architecture, too."

Renae didn't miss a beat. She selected a loose-leaf tea and spooned it into a silver tea diffuser, then poured hot water into her cup. "As you can probably tell, I've always liked the aesthetic."

Emma rejoined her at the table. She had such a big knot in her stomach she didn't think she could even take a sip of tea. But to keep Renae from thinking anything was amiss, she selected a tea and poured water into her cup. As Emma nervously dunked the diffuser, she tried to think of the best way to get Renae to talk about the assassination. All her rehearsals came to naught, because right at that second she decided flat-out was the way to go. Unfortunately she couldn't think of anything else, so she just went for it.

"You were present the night the president and the governor were killed, right?"

Renae's spine stiffened. "It isn't a subject I like to discuss."

"That's a problem," Emma said. "Then tell me about the painting."

Renae paled. "It's just a painting. Try one of these little lemon cakes, they're deli—"

"No, it's a painting of a time-share villa the...*killer* was supposed to be visiting the weekend of the murder."

"Pure coincidence," Renae insisted. "As we told the authorities twenty years ago, we sent out thousands of invitations from a mailing list we bought from a financial institution."

"We?"

"My husband and I were ready to develop the property so we were pre-selling vacation units. Cake? Sandwich?" she asked, passing the three-tiered plate in Emma's direction.

Emma took something that had cucumber in it and placed it, untouched, on her plate. "So there was no connection between your time-shares and the murders?"

"Why, of course not. Except for the fact that the assassin used the time-share invitation as part of his ruse. The rally was open to the public and well publicized, so he must have been planning the crime for a while. In fact, my husband was wounded in the attack. Can we please change the subject?"

"Sorry," Emma said, though not with much empathy. Something didn't feel right. Too many coincidences and she didn't really believe in coincidences.

Emma nibbled on a few sandwiches. Listened as Renae suggested places for her to visit and shop in the area. Basically, she was bored into a coma until Renae left to make a phone call.

Emma went back to the picture and looked at it again, taking a seat in one of the upholstered chairs before it. It was a stunning rendition and she decided she should go out to the place and see it for herself. Maybe something there would help her understand what had happened all those years ago. The ballistics report would help, but she still had no idea why her father had opened fire, or whether the president was in fact the intended target.

As she was trying to figure that out, Renae returned.

She wasn't alone. Just to her right, Kenny Simms was pointing a rather large gun in her direction.

"Get up," Kenny said.

Emma stood slowly, slipping her purse over her shoulder as she rose. "What is this?"

"Spare me," Renae said without the pretext of her southern charm and ever-present smile. "I know who you are. Kenny will take care of you first and then tomorrow, we'll dispatch your sister."

"Amelia doesn't know anything," Emma argued as Kenny roughly gripped her upper arm.

"I know," Kenny said. "I spent most of last night proving that. Your sister has a pretty high tolerance for pain."

Emma was temporarily blinded by fury. The thought that she was sharing space with Kenny Simms after what he'd done to Amelia was infuriating. She wanted to shoot him, then stand over him and shoot him a second time. She was seeing red along with the barrel of the gun.

"I still don't understand," Emma said to Renae. "How did you get my father involved in this?"

Renae shrugged. "He was just a convenient patsy."

"To kill a president?"

Renae sighed. "No, to kill the governor."

"But wasn't he your brother?"

"Yes. But that didn't stop him from being a thorn in my side. He was about to sign legislation that would have killed the Pine Landing project. Maddison and I had almost all of our cash tied into that project and my own brother was about to sign a law turning a big hunk of that property into protected wetlands."

"You killed three people over a land deal?" Emma asked softly. Her head was spinning. She'd believed her father was a killer for most of her life and now she was faced with an ugly truth. She'd accepted that fact without ever questioning the investigation. *Daddy, I'm so sorry!*

CHAPTER TWENTY-ONE

I'll come back for her car when I'm done," Simms said as he yanked Emma toward the door.

She practically tripped trying to keep up with his longer strides but most of her efforts were focused on keeping her small purse tucked beneath her arm.

"This way," he said as he half-dragged her across the lawn.

"Won't Mary notice that you dragged me out of the house?"

"Mary doesn't question what goes on here."

"You should. You were a cop. You know this is wrong."

"I know this pays better than being a state trooper," he replied.

They entered a side door to the multi-car garage and there was the shiny black Crown Victoria. Kenny pulled a fob from his pocket, pressed a button and the trunk opened slowly. "Get in."

"In the trunk?" Emma said, trying anything to buy some time as she slipped her hand into her purse.

"I can't watch you and drive at the same time. Now, get in."

It wasn't his menacing glare that made her comply; it was his large gun, with his beefy finger against the trigger. There wasn't a lot of room because of tools and other items strewn about, but if she bent her legs, she easily fit inside the compartment.

Fumbling around in the pitch dark of the confined space, she then snapped open her purse. The first thing she did was use the flashlight feature on her phone to scope out her situation. She spotted the red emergency lever and thought about yanking it and opening the trunk. But it didn't feel like the car was moving that fast and if she popped the trunk and made a run for it, Kenny could easily shoot her before she got ten feet away.

Emma paid attention as the car maneuvered. The sound of the gravel driveway beneath the tires gave way to a smooth ride after the car made a left. They were headed west of the Burke home. Unfortunately, she didn't know the area well enough to know what else might be west of the Burke home.

Quickly, she dialed Conner's number. "I've been kidnapped by Kenny Simms," she said in a quiet rush.

"Where are you?"

"In the trunk of his Crown Vic headed west."

"Are you hurt?"

"No, but I'm pretty sure that's phase two of this operation. Wait, the car is slowing down." Emma went silent and her attention was drawn to the left turn signal light, which she could see was flashing. She placed the phone on the floor for a second, just so she could remove one shoe.

Using the heel of her shoe like a hammer, she was able to knock out the taillight, allowing the fading daylight to stream into the trunk. "I can't see anything but passing cars," she told Conner with disappointment.

"I'm in the car now," he said. "What do you see?"

Kenny turned left and she felt the *thump-thump* of the tires against the highway. "I can't see much. Pine trees and scrub palms. No houses but I can feel and hear the uneven joints in the road. I think he may be taking me back to that logging road where he held Amelia."

"Are you sure?" Conner asked with concern.

"I'd say fifty-fifty," she admitted. "But I have a plan."

"Don't do anything to antagonize him," Conner said. "Just try to keep him talking."

"I'll do my best." She set her phone to voice recording and slipped it back into her purse, then drew her gun.

Even in the dim light she could see her hands shaking. Not good. Emma took several deep breaths and rolled so that she was half on her side, and her outstretched arms were partially hidden by the lip of the trunk latch.

She could feel the wheels leave the paved road and bounce over the ruts of the logging road. Hopefully it was the same logging road where they'd found Amelia. At least that way, she knew Conner had a chance of finding her. But would he be in time?

The resounding and immediate answer to that question was a big N-O. The car jerked to a stop and Emma braced herself and tried to steady her nerves. No small task when she heard the sound of the keys being pulled from the ignition, followed by the opening and closing of the driver's door.

From her self-made peephole, she saw Kenny as he rounded the car, and heard him cursing under his breath when he noticed the damaged taillight. She heard a small pop and the trunk lid slowly opened.

As soon as she saw Kenny's chest, she lifted her hands and fired. Twice.

Scrambling to her feet, she hit her head on the trunk, but kept her weapon trained on Kenny. He had a spreading crimson stain on the front of his shirt. His gun was still in his right hand, the keys in the other.

Ignoring the gun, Emma grabbed the keys and raced to the car door. She slipped behind the wheel and with her gun in her left hand, she attempted to insert the key. Unfortunately, her adrenaline was pumping and her hand was shaking so badly that she couldn't master the simple task. Her ears were pounding from the sound of close-quarter gunfire, but she kept struggling to start the engine.

Out of the corner of her eye she sensed movement. She looked up and was stunned to see Kenny standing next to the window, his gun raised.

Reflexively Emma raised her own gun and simultaneously heard a shot. She squeezed her eyes shut, waiting for the pain to hit. Nothing. Opening her eyes and looking down, she couldn't find a wound. Then suddenly the door was yanked open and she raised her gun again.

"It's me," Conner said as he gripped the barrel of her twenty-two and pushed it aside. "Are you hurt?"

She shook her head and started to cry. She didn't know why. Emma never cried. Then again, she'd never shot anyone before, either.

Conner gathered her in his arms and held her, stroking her hair. Sirens sounded in the distance. Emma gulped back her emotions and dabbed at her eyes with the backs of her hands. "C'mon," she said.

"Where? This is an officer-involved shooting. Protocol says—"

"Screw protocol. Renae Burke set this up and I want to watch you put that bitch in handcuffs."

Conner radioed in while Emma retrieved her purse from the open trunk. She glanced once at Kenny's prone body lying in the pine straw with a bullet between his eyes. "Nice shot," she commented as she and Conner went to the SUV to wait for the authorities.

Emma explained everything Renae had admitted. "My father wasn't the killer."

Conner reached out and squeezed her hand. "That's good, right?"

"Unless you count all the years I thought the worst of him."

"Don't beat yourself up about it. And call Amelia to let her know what's going on."

Amelia took the news quietly. She was probably feeling the same guilt Emma was. That couldn't be helped.

"Em?" Amelia began tentatively.

"Yeah?"

"I spoke to Mom's nurse a little while ago. It doesn't look good."

"Is she conscious?"

"In and out."

"I'll book two flights for tomorrow morning. We'll go home as soon as they let you out of the hospital."

"I don't know when that will be," Amelia argued.

"We'll use a charter if we have to. You just rest and I'll call you as soon as Renae is arrested."

"So who was the second man?" Amelia asked.

"Are you sure you can recognize his voice?" Emma asked.

"Absolutely."

"Then I'll have a tape of Maddison Burke for you tonight."

"Maddison?" Conner asked.

Emma nodded. "Who else had a stake in that development property? And I can't imagine Renae trusting just anyone."

"When I go in there, you can't make a scene," he warned.

"I may gloat."

Conner offered her a smile. "You've earned that, I suppose."

After meeting with various officials, she and Conner were free to leave. They got in the SUV and headed back to Purdue. In no time, they turned up Renae's drive. Emma's car was still parked in the front of the house.

At the front door, Conner pressed the bell and Mary answered. "Sheriff, Miss McKinley."

"Is Mrs. Burke in?"

"She's in the parlor."

"Not for long," Emma muttered under her breath.

As soon as they crossed the threshold, Renae's eyes grew as wide as dinner plates at the sight of Emma. "What—?"

"Kenny didn't make it," Emma said.

"Renae Burke?" Conner confirmed as he took his handcuffs off the back of his utility belt.

"There has to be some sort of mistake, Sheriff. I don't know what this woman has told you but anything Kenny did, he did of his own accord."

Emma scoffed. "You brought him in here and ordered him to kill me."

"Nonsense. You're hysterical." Then Renae apparently read the look on Connor's face, because she said less stridently, "I refuse to be carted away like a common criminal! Let me call my attorney; he'll sort this out."

"You can do that after you're booked," Conner informed her as cuffed her. "Where's your husband?"

"He'll be home any minute."

"Good," Emma said. "I need a favor from him."

Renae glared at her. "I believe I'll exercise my right to remain silent now."

No sooner had Renae shut up than a flustered Maddison came bursting into the room demanding, "What is the meaning of this?"

"Hang on," Emma said, taking her phone out of her

purse. She pressed the voice record button. "Your wife tried to have me killed today."

"That's ludicrous."

"She also told me all about the time-share and the governor's threat to turn your property into a worthless investment. I know you set my father up."

"You're forgetting something, young lady. I was shot that night, too."

"Probably part of the cover-up," Emma surmised.

"Sheriff, I insist that you uncuff my wife immediately."

"That's not going to happen. In fact, I'll need you to turn around and put your hands behind your back."

"You have got to be kidding."

Conner produced a second set of cuffs. "Does this look like I'm kidding?"

Seeing them both in handcuffs went a long way toward making Emma feel better.

* * *

It had been three weeks since she'd left Purdue. That time had been filled with reflection, sadness, and annoyance. Her mother had lived just long enough to hear that her husband had not been an assassin. Though her passing had been expected, Emma was still saddened when the time came. The media had been unrelenting in their requests for interviews and cameras seemed to follow them everywhere they went. It got so bad that Emma and Amelia finally agreed to a nationally televised interview by a major network, and that seemed to satisfy the public's need to know all the gory details.

The reflection occupied her mind at every possible turn. After many sleepless nights and many more conversations with Amelia, Emma finally realized what she needed to do. With her sister's blessing, she called Elgin Hale and got her job back.

Conner hadn't called her except to offer condolences when her mother passed, and as much as she wanted to call him, she wasn't sure where they stood. But she knew the easiest way to let him know she was back in town.

On her first morning back, she got up extra early and went to Stella's for breakfast. She got a few stares while she sat at a table, sipping coffee and waiting for her omelet.

Though she ate slowly, there were still no signs of Conner. *Great time for the Purdue gossip mill to go down.* So she walked the two blocks to her office and was welcomed back with open arms. Her arms weren't so open after a few minutes, however. Elgin loaded her down with casework and she found herself inside her office, reviewing files.

The day flew by and by its end Emma was practically seeing double from reading so many booking documents and pleadings. Everyone else was long gone, save for Elgin. Emma saw the light on under his door when she went to make a fresh pot of coffee.

She had turned back from filling the machine with water when she spotted a figure in the doorway. She was so startled that she dropped the carafe and it shattered against the tile floor. There'd be office mutiny, but that didn't matter.

She could only focus on the fact that Conner Kavanaugh, in a suit no less, filled the doorway. His sexy half-smile sent her pulse racing. "Welcome back," he said.

"How do you know I'm here to stay?"

"Jeanine told Peggy, who works at the market, who's married to the mechanic who services the department's vehicles, and he told me."

"Good to know Purdue is maintaining its charm."

"What about me?" he asked. "Have I retained my charm?"

Except for his furrowed brow, he looked wonderful. "What's wrong?"

"They postponed my brother's parole hearing. Drove up there today for no reason."

"I'm sorry," Emma said as she stepped over the shattered glass. "I have a few things for you in my office." She took him by the hand and led him back to her desk. "This," she paused and took a thick stack of pages out of her briefcase, "is case law dating practically back to the Civil War that your brother's attorney can use to support his parole request. And this"—she pulled out another voluminous pack—"is a Request to Modify Custody and Visitation."

"When did you have time to do all this?"

"When I was in Georgia. You really need to run the custody thing past Sam."

"Well, she'll do anything if it means spending more time with David."

"Are they in love?" Emma asked with a sly grin.

Conner came around her desk and pulled her into his embrace. He kissed her hard and urgently. Her body responded immediately. Her heart quickened, her nerves tingled and she had an overwhelming urge to rip the clothes from his body.

The kiss ended as abruptly as it began. Emma was so unsteady she wound up falling into her chair. "Wow, that was a great kiss."

Conner stepped back around the desk. "Which is why I'm putting some space between us."

"There's no one here but Elgin and I can lock my office door," she suggested.

"Which is why I'm on this side of the desk. We have to talk but if I get within a few feet of you, talking is the last thing on my mind."

Emma shrugged. "So talk." She smiled at him. "Quickly."

"I've done nothing but think about you for the last three weeks. But I come with baggage. I have a daughter."

"Who I think is terrific and who I believe likes me."

"She does. Then there's the difference in our balance sheets."

Emma rolled her eyes. "Having money is rarely a problem. Not having it can tear people apart."

"Do we keep separate houses or consolidate?"

Emma laughed. "How about we figure all that out on our second date?"

"There's that, too. Technically, we've only been on one date."

"So let's start there. I have a feeling everything else will fall into place." Emma stood and walked around the desk and got up on tiptoe to kiss his chin. "I have something to say, too."

"What?"

"I'm pretty sure I love you."

He reached up and cupped her face in his hands. "I'm more than pretty sure," he said, then he kissed her deeply.

PLEASE TURN THE PAGE
FOR A PREVIEW OF TRAPPED,
THE THIRD BOOK IN
RHONDA POLLERO'S EXHILARATING
FINDING JUSTICE SERIES,
AVAILABLE IN FALL 2017.

PROLOGUE

Chasyn Summers parked her Prius on the street adjacent to the courthouse on East Ocean Boulevard. Her best friend and witness, Kasey, was belted into the passenger's side.

"Are you nervous?" Kasey asked.

Chasyn thought for a minute while she checked her make-up in the rearview mirror. The state's attorney had warned them to wear subdued clothing and modest make-up. Something about making them seem more sympathetic to the grand jury. So she had chosen a navy skirt and a cream-colored blouse and she had forgone eye makeup save for a touch of mascara and applied just a hint of blush-nude lipstick to complete the look. Her blond hair was pulled tight into a neat ponytail. She couldn't look more matronly if she tried. "I feel like a school marm."

"Tell me about it. I spent over a hundred dollars on this dress and it really needs to be hemmed. After we testify, I'll take it to the seamstress and have her turn it into a proper little black dress."

"Well, for now we are not two twentysomethings out at a bar at two a.m., we're upstanding citizens who witnessed a murder."

Kacey shivered. "I still have nightmares about that."

"Me, too," Chasyn said. "But at least this will help them arrest Dr. Lansing. Thanks to us, or more specifically you."

"Should be a cakewalk," Kasey said. "Except remember, the state's attorney said the defense attorney would probably attack both of us because we'd been drinking that night."

"Hours earlier and only two drinks. I mean how many times does a girl turn twenty-nine?" Chasyn asked. "We were both stone-cold sober when we walked out of that restaurant and found that poor girl on the pavement." She smoothed a wayward hair. "Ready?"

"Sure," they exited the car and walked the short distance to the court house. It was two buildings separated by a breezeway. Chasyn knew from earlier meetings with the state's attorney that they wanted to be on the left side of the Martin County, Florida, courthouse.

As they approached the buildings, she heard a loud pop and suddenly found herself falling forward. A split second later she heard a second pop and Kasey fell next to her. Kasey's eyes were open but blood was trickling out of her mouth.

Chasyn was vaguely aware of people screaming. People running. Then she felt wetness and saw a pool of blood starting to form around her face. She smelled burned flesh and a distinct ringing in her ears.

After what seemed like a long time, someone came over to her and whispered, "You've been shot in the head. Try not to move."

About the Author

After selling her first work of romantic suspense in 1993, Rhonda Pollero has penned more than thirty novels, won numerous awards and nominations, and landed on multiple bestseller lists, including *USA Today*, Bookscan, and Ingram's Top 50 list. She lives in South Florida with her family.